CREATURES OF

MAGIC

carolyn
Stowe

10 nelson street gordon
sydney Australia

CREATURES of
MAGIC

❋

Maree Fenton-Smith
Illustrated by Lilly Piri

WALKER BOOKS
AND SUBSIDIARIES

LONDON • BOSTON • SYDNEY • AUCKLAND

First published in 2013
by Walker Books Australia Pty Ltd
Locked Bag 22, Newtown
NSW 2042 Australia
www.walkerbooks.com.au

The moral rights of the author and illustrator have been asserted.

National Library of Australia Cataloguing-in-Publication entry:
Fenton-Smith, Maree, 1963– author.
Creatures of magic / Maree Fenton-Smith; illustrator Lilly Piri.
ISBN: 978 1 922077 73 8 (paperback)
For primary school age.
Subjects: Witches – Juvenile fiction.
          Neighbors – Juvenile fiction.
Other Authors/Contributors: Piri, Lilly, illustrator.
A823.4

The illustrations for this book were created with graphite pencil and charcoal
Typeset in Centaur MT
Printed and bound in China

For my own Creatures of Magic –
Zoe, Ella, Milly and Charlie. MFS

For Heiko, Mum, Dad, Tarynt, and my
favourite creatures, Gilligan and Sam.
Ad astra per alas porci. LP

1

Fairytale, *noun* a story with magical creatures in it;
an account of a strange incident.

This is a fairytale with no fairies in it. This is not unusual. Have you noticed how many fairytales don't have fairies? Take *Snow White* — definitely no fairies there. *Hansel and Gretel* — again, no fairies. The common factor in most of the fairytales I have read (and I have read many) is the presence of witches, and this is what my story has in abundance. There is also some blood, gore and violence (in the context of a PG-rated movie rather than an M-rated one), some evil, no small amount of creepiness and a bit of misunderstanding between the characters that is eventually cleared up (mostly).

So this story has a happyish ending. This won't surprise you if you know your fairytales. The goodies generally win and the baddies come to a sticky end and luckily in real life this sometimes happens as well. And that tells you the most interesting thing about this fairytale. It is the real-life story of what happened to me over the summer holidays when I was eleven.

Even though I am the narrator of this story, I am also a main character so I will tell you a little bit about myself. My name is Anna and I live with my parents and my eight-year-old sister Greta in a location that I cannot divulge because of the sensitive nature of this story.

We live in an old two-storey (three if you count the attic) terrace. The lounge room, kitchen and bathroom are downstairs and all the bedrooms are upstairs. Our street is in a suburb that is made up of lots of terraces and trees, and my primary school is just at the end of my street.

As for me, I wear glasses. I have red hair, freckles and a double-jointed elbow. I am not and never have been an orphan. Most girls with red hair in books and movies are orphans (Anne of Green Gables, Annie, and Pippi Longstocking to name a few). Why is this so?

I like reading. I even like reading the dictionary. Some of my friends think this is strange but my mother tells me not to worry about it, that people might laugh now, but it is something that will stand me in good stead later in life. My favourite word is "crevasse". I love it because it is a pointy word which makes me think of graceful snow-capped mountains — the opposite of what it is — a crevasse is a dangerous, deep hidden gully covered by snow and is treacherous to mountaineers.

I prefer apples to bananas, and I would like to live in a house in the country with lots of dogs, a horse and some cute baby triplet sisters (one for me, one for my sister Greta and one for Mum and Dad). But that kind of detail is not really so important.

The important thing is the magic, and the magic came with our new next-door neighbours, the Browns, who arrived on the last day of school.

Our old neighbours had left earlier in the year and we had all been waiting eagerly to see who would move in next. Our houses shared a wall so we were keen for our new neighbours to be people we liked.

Our old neighbours were a quiet family of three, Mrs Rita Raton and her two children. I never knew what happened to Mr Raton — he did not live next door and didn't visit. No one visited. The children, Emily and Edward, were younger than Greta. They never played or fought with each other like we did, and we never saw them in their backyard. Sometimes, jumping on our trampoline, I looked up and saw Emily's unhappy face pressed against one of the upstairs windows. When I waved she quickly moved away.

Mum and I once packed up some of Greta's and my old clothes

and toys, ones that were still in good condition, and took them over to the Ratons' place. But they were returned to our doorstep the same day, with a note saying they weren't needed. Mrs Raton was a note writer rather than a talker. She wrote notes to Mum and Dad about the fence (should be higher), my cat Ginger (keep him out of her backyard) and the noise we made (should be less).

I was hoping the new family would have children – noisy children who wanted to play at our house, preferably girl children around the age of eleven. Maybe there would be a couple of them, one for me and one for Greta, so we didn't have to share friends. None of my friends lived close to school like me, and my best friend Lydia usually spent the holidays travelling somewhere exciting like Thailand with her family, so school holidays could be lonely.

Lydia's school holiday arrangements had done wonders for my vocabulary. I started reading the dictionary last summer when I ran out of books. Mum would not take me to the library until I found every overdue book at our house. I couldn't.

In desperation I raided Mum and Dad's bookshelf and found an old dictionary Mum had used at school, as well as some grown-up books about mountaineering and Antarctica that turned out to be really interesting. I pretty much exhausted Mum and Dad's bookshelf last summer holidays though. I dreamed about having a friend that I could climb over the fence to talk to, rather than having to plan it with Mum. We didn't have to be *best* friends. We could hang out together when we felt like it. Sometimes you just had to make do with what was available – like the books on the bookshelf last summer. I would never have chosen those books from the library, but they'd been a great read. I was hoping the new neighbours would be like this – the "person" equivalent of a great read.

❋

In some fairytales, the arrival of the Browns would have been preceded by some mysterious event or circumstance, like a black-hooded crone lurking on the street corner, droning on about doom and disaster through the haze of fog and rain. But this didn't happen, not that I noticed anyway.

The day the Browns moved in next door was bright and hot, and their arrival was heralded by a removal truck that blocked half the street. The only mutterings of discontent came from people trying to park their cars, mutterings that changed to murmurings of curiosity once the truck started unloading. A parade of rodents, some of them large, and all of them dead, were the first things carried in by the removal men. They were not friendly rodents. Even had they been alive, rather than preserved and stuffed, they were not the kind of creatures that could ever have been pets. They were wild animals, or at least had been wild animals.

Mum, hurrying me and Greta to school, paused to stare. "Taxidermy?" she asked no one in particular, frowning and screwing up her nose.

"What's taxidermy?" asked Greta. "And are those animals dead? How gross!"

"Taxidermy means stuffed animals," I explained. One advantage of dictionary reading was that it made me seem knowledgeable. Not that Greta always respected this knowledge. "And, yes, they are dead. It used to be trendy for people to have their pets stuffed when they died. I think it was so they could keep them forever and wouldn't miss them so much."

"That's no pet," said Greta as one of the removalists carried in a particularly fierce-looking marsupial rat, and I agreed. The removalist paused to smile at our shocked faces.

"Bit creepy, aren't they?" he said. One of his teeth had a gold cap on the tip and it glinted in the sunlight, below his black mustache. "There's more good stuff coming, girls, believe me!"

And he was right. Luckily, the phone rang. While Mum went inside to answer it, Greta and I hung around the front gate,

watching the removalists. After the taxidermic rodents came a massive cage with a blanket thrown over it, large enough to house a small horse. The wheels on the cage were rusty and creaked with the effort of rotation. It was a grating noise, and whatever was inside the cage sounded irritated. A low, menacing growl, muffled by the blanket, travelled through the air. The four men stopped pushing the cage and picked it up, grunting.

"Through the side gate, straight to the yard. Steady on, boys!" the man with the gold tooth said sharply as the cage started to vibrate. The men steadied on, the cage stabilised and the growling stopped. I heard a snuffling sound as the cage went past.

"Wow, what was that? A horse?" asked Greta.

"Horses don't growl," I said thoughtfully, and Greta and I started to giggle at the silliness of a horse moving into the terrace next door.

We were late for school that day. The stuff coming off the removal truck was just too exciting. After the stuffed rodents and the large growling cage, the removalists had unpacked five smaller cages, each containing dozens of mice: fat, sleek mice running over each other, some white and some brown.

"Do you think they're pets?" Greta asked. She was very fond of her three pet mice, Sugar, Marmalade and Fuzzy.

"I don't know," I puzzled. The mice looked very well cared for but there was something about the amount of them that was sinister, and that didn't seem quite pet-like. I was glad Mum was inside on the phone. I knew she wouldn't be happy about the number of mice moving in with our new neighbours.

After the cages of mice came a mannequin, some statues and lots of rectangular boxes. "Think they've packed a library," the man with the gold tooth complained as he walked past with another box. Then came paintings, mostly of animals. They weren't pictures of happy cows in paddocks though; they were uncomfortable pictures of cats watching mice, heavy oil paintings of cats on their own looking sulky.

Mum arrived back in time to see the harp. It was good timing — she liked music more than mice. She looked with interest at the large harp before hurrying us up the hill to school. "It will all be here when you get home this afternoon," she chided. "You are going to be so late!"

Not that being late mattered in the last week of school, which was more about packing up and doing fun Christmassy things than schoolwork. Saying goodbye to Lydia who was leaving the next day was hard, and I didn't have time to think about our new neighbours until we got home. It was only after we sat down and had a cold drink that I questioned Mum about the new people next door.

"Have they arrived yet?" I asked, thinking that the people who belonged with the possessions we'd seen that morning would have to be interesting.

"They have indeed," said Mum. "With children, you'll be pleased to know, and cats — I've seen at least four so far. I've heard them playing outside. It makes a change hearing noisy children out there."

I ran outside to climb the tree that overlooked our new neighbours' backyard. Greta was already up the tree — she climbed fast.

I loved the garden next door. Although our houses were kind of like twins, there were small differences, and the garden was one of them. It was a lot more overgrown than ours, with more trees and vines than garden beds. Dad said it was a breeding ground for mosquitoes, and I could see what the mozzies liked about the place. There was a jacaranda tree with a bright pink bougainvillea climbing through it and a tangle of jasmine that ran along the fence.

I could see a woman bent over a garden bed with a tub of strawberries in her hand. Our cat Ginger had made himself at home lolling around our new neighbour's feet.

"Hello," Greta called out before I had a chance to get a proper look. "Hullo, my name's Greta," she called again when there was no response from the woman.

"Hello Greta," said the woman, looking up. She had a round brown face with greeny eyes — cat's eyes, Greta and I later agreed. She was dressed in an old sundress decorated with a silver cat's head brooch. She yawned and it turned into a smile.

"My name's Pamela Brown. Do you want to come over and meet the kids? Violet and Tabitha would love to play with someone who wasn't a brother or sister. I think they're all getting a bit sick of each other's company with the move and being cooped up in the car for so long. And it was a long trip before we got into the car."

Mum was watering the garden. As we rushed down to ask whether we could go, she was picking a bunch of flowers for the new neighbours.

"Yes, yes, you can go." She laughed. "Take these over for them. Wait a moment and I'll get you a vase, they probably haven't unpacked that kind of stuff. Don't hang around for too long. I'm sure they have a million things to do and it probably won't help to have two extra children underfoot. Why don't you ask the girls whether they would like to play over here?"

"Yes, Mum," we said.

But we had no intention of asking the Brown girls over to our house, not that afternoon anyway. Not with that big house to explore and all those interesting boxes. And mice. I took the flowers from Mum before she could remind me to put my shoes on, and Greta and I quickly climbed over the fence rather than bothering to go around the front. From my brief look at Mrs Brown I felt that she was not the kind of person to get hung up about kids without shoes climbing over her back fence.

I had a good feeling about these new neighbours with their harp, books, mice and cats.

2

Tincture, *noun* an old-fashioned potion made with flowers or herbs, used as medicine in the olden days.

"Hi, Mrs Brown," we said. I felt suddenly shy and gave the flowers to Greta who shrugged and handed them to Mrs Brown.

"Here you go," she said.

"Mum gave us these to give to you," I added. I didn't really like talking to new people, but it didn't feel right that Greta did all the talking.

"Why thank you, girls – how sweet! I absolutely love flowers, and please call me Pamela." Pamela had a face that looked at home in a smile. Close up you realised how green her eyes were. Her hair was brown and curly in a messy kind of way, with lots of grey running through it, and her fingernails were dirty, probably from her recent gardening. She was very tall. There was something about Pamela that took my shyness away.

She sniffed the flowers deeply and then held them out in front of her. A silver leather bracelet was buckled on her wrist and as she looked at the flowers a small bell attached to it tinkled.

"Does your mother use pesticides?" she asked.

"What?" asked Greta.

"No!" I said.

I watched in wonder as Pamela tore off a handful of the flower petals and popped them into her mouth. "Delish," she said, munching away with some of the stems caught between her teeth. She tore another handful off and chewed with relish. Greta and I watched in fascination. She ate the flowers like a horse eats grass, tearing the petals and not worrying much about closing her mouth as she chewed.

"Thanks, girls," Pamela said, wiping a brown hand across her green mouth. "What with the move and unpacking I hadn't thought about food. And nasturtiums are so nutritious. Great in tinctures as well. Delectable! I probably should have left some for the girls, not that Violet is keen on flowers – ironic given her name really. Come inside and I'll try to find them for you."

Pamela took our hands firmly and led us up the back steps into the house.

Although the exterior of the two terraces looked similar, the interior was very different. Ours had had quite a few walls knocked out, so downstairs was only two big rooms, including the kitchen, whereas the Browns' downstairs had lots of small rooms with closed doors. After watching the way Pamela Brown ate the flowers I felt sure there would be some surprises behind the closed doors. The floorboards were a dullish grey colour, very different to our shiny brown boards, and the walls had paint peeling off in some places. There was unpacked crockery in the kitchen and there were half-opened boxes everywhere. The paintings we had seen earlier were resting against the walls and I could see some of the larger taxidermic animals standing in a group in the lounge room.

"I think the girls must be upstairs, decorating their bedroom," Pamela said. "Here, why don't you take these cupcakes upstairs to them? I'm sure they must be hungry."

"Are we allowed to eat them upstairs?" asked Greta, doubtfully.

"Oh yes," said Pamela. She must have read the surprise in our faces because she added, "Don't worry, Tabitha has mice that will make quick work of the crumbs."

"You do have a lot of mice," I said, taking the offered plate of cupcakes from Pamela, glad she hadn't handed me any bushes from the garden for afternoon tea.

"Violet's cats make sure our mouse population remains stable. We all try to help each other in our family." Pamela smiled reassuringly at Greta and me.

Greta was not reassured. "Does she mean Violet's cats eat Tabitha's mice?" she whispered to me as we climbed up the stairs.

"I think so," I said.

I wondered what kind of sisters Violet and Tabitha were, to share their pets so wholeheartedly with one another, sacrificing one for the sake of a meal for the other. Did it mean they loved each other so much they were happy to make that sacrifice, or was Tabitha simply not very fond of her pet mice?

I held Greta's hand. It felt very dark after the sunlight outside and I could see bright patches dancing in front of me. Everything smelled dusty and a bit stale. The Browns' house had even more small rooms upstairs than down.

Boxes lined one of the hallways upstairs, some of them open. I saw books in one of the boxes and bent over to look more closely. Some had thick, heavy padded covers with gold writing that seemed to glow in the dark of the stairwell. I touched the writing — it felt warm and my fingertips lingered. There was a honeyish kind of smell. As I moved closer to see whether it was coming from the book, I heard a clear voice say, "Don't touch the books."

I turned around, scared. I knew I hadn't done anything wrong, but I could feel my heart beating.

"Sorry," I muttered. As my eyes became more accustomed to

the dark I could make out the form of a girl standing on the first landing.

"Who goes there?" asked the girl. She said it in a curious, rather than abrupt, way and her voice was soft. She had black hair tied back in a ponytail and her eyes were an unusual shade of green. She was wearing shorts and a T-shirt. A silver cat's head brooch, similar to the one her mother wore, was pinned to it. The brooch had small green stones for eyes and it looked antique, something my grandmother would wear pinned to a dress rather than something that belonged on a girl's T-shirt.

"I'm Anna. I live next door," I said, walking closer to the girl. She had an elastic bracelet wrapped twice and buckled around her wrist, with a small bell attached to it. Three cats were rubbing themselves against her legs. "Are those all your cats?" I asked.

She glanced down as though she hadn't noticed there were any cats there.

"No," she said, and looking more closely I realised that our cat, Ginger, who wasn't very sociable at the best of times, was one of her admirers.

"Ginger," I said, "come on, boy." He ignored me, leisurely chewing on a mouse that half-dangled from his mouth, then dropped it at the girl's feet.

"Bad Ginger!" said Greta. She bent down to look at the mouse.

"It's passed on," said the girl, picking it up. "I think it's one of Tabitha's." She looked at it in an appraising way and for one awful moment I thought she was going to pop it in her mouth and eat it, just like her mother had eaten the flowers, but she dropped it at the last moment. She turned and walked into the room at the top of the stairs.

She whispered something to Ginger. Ginger followed her into the room, ignoring Greta and me.

"Enter," said the girl. "Just watch out for the mice."

She called into the room, "Tabitha, careful — guests approaching."

I stepped forwards cautiously. These people were exciting but in a crevasse-like way — unpredictable and potentially treacherous.

3

Pet, *noun* **tame animal you love, look after and don't eat.**

Greta grabbed my hand. Normally it was me needing to hold Greta's hand so I knew she was feeling apprehensive as we entered the room.

"Seal the exit," the girl ordered.

I shut the door and the girl shuddered at the loud sound.

There were mice everywhere. They were crawling over full boxes and into empty ones. In one corner of the room a seething, moving carpet of brown was making its way into a small hole in the wall. It was like peak hour at a train station, with the mice steadily moving in one stream towards the exit point.

"Aren't they your pets?" Greta asked the two girls. "Do you want us to help you catch them and put them away?"

"No, they're probably safer in the wall," said the younger of the two girls. She had dark hair like her sister's, tied in pigtails. She had freckles and greenish eyes with brown flecks in them.

"The cats keep sleeping on the mouse cage and putting their paws in so I think it's only fair to give them a decent chance at life," said the younger girl, yawning.

"Why don't you just put them somewhere away from the cats, where they can't get at them?" I asked.

Tabitha and Violet (as I later came to know them) looked at me with pity. "What's the fun in that for the cats?" Violet asked.

It was on the tip of my tongue to point out that the mice could hardly enjoy their combined role as toy and lunch for the cats, but I was distracted by the fact that despite the abundance of mice in the room, the cats were not showing the slightest bit of interest. Ginger was washing his face with his paws and, as I watched, a mouse jumped over his head, brushing Ginger's whiskers with his tail. Even this provocative and disrespectful behaviour failed to draw a response from Ginger.

"Have they been eating mice all morning?" I asked, cringing as I watched the lounging cats.

"No, I just told them to give the mice a break for a while," said Violet.

"And they listen to you?" asked Greta.

"Attentively," said Violet, flicking her dark hair.

"Oh, right, so you speak cat, do you?" I asked. Was she making fun of me? It was difficult to feel shy and irritated at the same time, and these girls' claims were irritating. I lost my usual shyness. I had an imagination but I wasn't gullible.

"Yes," said Violet, as though cat as a second language was something she learned at school. She yawned and Greta rolled her eyes at me.

"Keeping you up, are we?" Greta asked.

There was silence in the room, except for the sound of little claws scraping the wooden floorboards as the mice continued through the hole in the wall.

We all stared at each other and I felt my dream of next-door neighbourliness, sleepovers and play dates fading. I thought of the long summer holidays and Lydia being away, the dictionary already read and the most recent round of library books still not found.

"Tell Ginger he needs to start eating his dinner then," I said, trying to lighten the mood in the room. "He seems to have gone off his food a bit lately."

"If you wish," Violet said.

"Are those cupcakes?" queried Tabitha, noticing the plate that Pamela had given me.

"Let's partake," said Violet, taking the plate from me and

offering Greta, Tabitha and me the cupcakes before helping herself to one. Tabitha crumbled part of her cupcake near the stream of commuting mice. A small estuary broke away to eat the crumbs before resuming their procession towards the exit.

We all munched the cupcakes. I watched Violet take very small, neat mouthfuls. She left few crumbs for the mice, and I noticed again that the three cats in the room were all leaning against her.

Ginger's face had an expression of contentment I hadn't seen before. I made the kissing sound Ginger usually loved. "Gingerbread boy, come here," I said softly. He ignored me and jumped onto Violet's lap, rubbing the side of his face against one of her hands. I felt my face go red.

"So what year were you in at your old school?" I asked, deciding to follow my pet's lead of friendliness.

"Year Five," said Violet.

"Year Five going into Year Six?" I asked.

"Is there any other kind of Year Five?" Violet asked.

"Well, I suppose if you were repeating," said Tabitha. "Violet's not repeating," she added. "And I'm in Year Three going into Year Four. We're starting at the school up the road."

"If we're still here, Tabitha," said Violet. "Hopefully we won't be."

I looked at Violet. Her comments didn't indicate any need for friendship, that's for sure.

"That's our school," said Greta, ignoring Violet and focussing on Tabitha. "I'm going into Year Four as well. Maybe we'll be in the same class."

"What time does school start?" asked Tabitha. "I hope it's not too early."

"All schools around here start early, Tabitha," Violet answered quickly. "Probably around nine o'clock?" She looked to me for confirmation.

"Nine-fifteen," I said.

Tabitha groaned loudly. "That's ridiculous!" she said. "I'll never be able to get up that early."

"What time did your old school start?" I asked.

Violet gave Tabitha a look I recognised — it was the same kind of look I often gave Greta. It was a "don't say anything or you're dead look".

She answered for Tabitha. "Our old school started later than that. We're not natural early risers in our family."

Ginger ate every skerrick of his dinner that night. I watched him

30

wolf it down, something he had not done for months. Afterwards, as he was cleaning his whiskers, he gave me his "so?" look, as if there was nothing at all unusual about his behaviour.

Was he following Violet's directions?

4

Confidant, *noun* person trusted with
private affairs; someone you tell secrets to.

"You're both very quiet," Mum commented during dinner. "How did it go next door?"

"Cat got your tongue?" teased Dad.

Greta and I looked at each other. We had wordlessly agreed to edit certain details of our visit next door. Although we had ended up having heaps of fun with Tabitha and Violet, catching mice and putting them back in their cages (Violet and Tabitha did most of the catching, but they let us play with the mice before we put them back), we knew Mum might have reservations about the plague-like proportions of mice next door. We'd left when Tabitha and Violet had curled up on the floor and gone to sleep, which had been odd. The number of mice and Pamela's eating of the flowers had been even odder. We knew the word "odd" would mean danger in Mum's mind. We wanted our time next door to continue, preferably with parental support, so we had kept our account of the afternoon brief. At least I was brief, and so was Greta, with the assistance of a couple of nudges from me.

"Well, you seem tired," Dad said, helping himself to some salad. "I'm enjoying the quiet. Keep up whatever exhausting activity you were engaged in next door, I say."

"Sure," agreed Greta.

"I'm very tired," I said, yawning and looking pointedly at Greta. "Do you mind if I go straight to bed?"

"No," said Mum and Dad in unison.

"Me too," said Greta, leaving the table. She yawned, sounding fake.

Mum raised her eyebrows. "Are you girls up to something?"

"Of course not," I said in what I hoped was a tired-sounding voice. "Night — love you." I took Greta's hand to ensure she walked up the stairs quietly.

During our afternoon next door we had worked out that our bedroom and the Brown girls' bedroom were side by side. We had also discovered that their bedroom, like ours, had an attic used for storage above it, accessed by a ladder that you pulled down from the ceiling. The most exciting discovery though had been that our attic and their attic had no wall separating them. This meant you could move from Violet and Tabitha's bedroom into ours via the roof space, as long as both ladders were down. We had agreed that we would all meet in the shared attic at 8.30pm. Not for any particular reason, but just because we could. I was hoping, in the darkness of the shared roof space, I could ask Violet some questions about her cat comments.

At the agreed time I heard a small *rat-a-tat-tat* on the ceiling. I pulled the attic ladder down as gently as I could, wincing at the loud squeaking. I so hoped Mum and Dad wouldn't be able to hear it from downstairs. Violet and Tabitha slunk down the ladder, and then quietly put it back up. I was struck by their agility and grace. I heard the soft tinkle of a bell and realised Violet was still wearing her elastic bracelet with the bell attached.

"Greetings." whispered Violet. I was dying to go up into the attic but I knew it was only fair that they check out our bedroom.

"Do you want to have a quick look around here?" I whispered. "Mum will come up to say goodnight soon, but you could hide under the bed and then when she's gone we could all go into the attic."

"If you wish," said Violet. "Neat as a pin – how lovely." She had recovered from her afternoon tiredness and was full of interest in everything. Looking at my collection of books, she pulled out a gilt-edged fairytale. She flicked through a couple of pages and put it back in place.

"It looks like a book of spells, although you can't judge a book by its cover," she commented.

"Yes," I said, wondering whether she was joking with me. "If spell books existed."

Violet said nothing. I was about to ask her what she knew about spells when I heard Mum on the stairs. I motioned for Violet and Tabitha to crawl under the bed.

"Are you all right, darling?" Mum asked, putting her hand on my forehead. "I hope you're not getting sick; you don't often feel so tired."

"She's fine, Mum!" Greta called from her bed.

"Yes, really I feel great," I said. I was acutely conscious of Violet and Tabitha under my bed. "But tired – great but tired at the same time," I added. "Tired in a physically-exhausted-from-jumping-so-much-on-the-trampoline kind of way."

"If Anna's sick, she won't be able to go next door tomorrow, will she?" Greta asked.

"Shut up, Greta!" I snapped.

"All right, girls, that's enough. Goodnight," Mum said. She seemed reassured by my snapping.

When I was sure Mum was settled on the couch again, I pulled down the attic ladder. At every squeak I expected to hear footsteps up the stairs, but the sound of Mum shouting at the television about unfair umpire decisions and Dad's more muffled agreement was comforting.

My heart was thumping as we climbed up the ladder, and it wasn't just because it was so dark up there. I was on the edge of something, something indefinable, something exciting, something dangerous. The air was tingling with the fizz of it and the fizz centred around Violet.

We sat companionably in cross-legged position on the floor. Tabitha had brought some bananas and she shared them with Greta. Was it the sloppy sound of bananas being chewed, or the butterflies in my stomach that were making me feel queasy? Greta and Tabitha were effectively gagged by having mouths full of banana. Violet was silent. It felt like she was waiting for me to talk. So I did.

"Today when we were talking," I started.

"Yes," she said.

I could feel her eyes looking at me in the dark and was glad I couldn't see them; they had a way of staring that could be uncomfortable.

"Well, you were talking about speaking cat and I was just wondering what you meant by that," I asked carefully.

She didn't answer straightaway. I could still hear Greta chewing banana and the smell of it made my stomach lurch.

"Greta, do you mind moving away with those bananas? It's making me feel sick." Tabitha had brought a small torch and they crawled away, guided by its tunnel of light, to a pile of stuff on the Browns' side of the attic, whispering together.

The silence that had been comfortable before was going on for too long. You could almost hear Violet thinking. I knew the question I'd asked was important, and I knew that Violet was wondering whether she could trust me. I wanted to show her I could be trusted. Maybe if I shared something personal with her, she would do the same with me?

"Do you like reading?" I asked. "What are your favourite books?"

"I like history books," said Violet. "Or books with recipes for tinctures, books that teach me useful things. I don't read that much." She did not elaborate on this and after another period of silence I tried again.

"I know this might sound funny," I said, "but my favourite books are fairytales. I like the creepy old-fashioned ones with magic." Violet didn't say anything. "Greta teases me about it," I said. "She says that it's babyish."

Violet didn't acknowledge that I had just told her something I usually kept to myself. I tried again.

"I read a lot," I said. "People don't believe how quickly I can read. Sometimes even my teachers don't believe me. I hate it when people think I'm lying when I say I've finished a book the day after I've borrowed it from the library. And some people think that I don't understand what some of the words I say mean."

I could feel Violet listening to me.

"What kind of words?" she asked.

"Words like crevasse," I said. "It's my favourite word. It's like a dangerous hidden valley in the snow."

We were both quiet. It was a comfortable, companionable kind of silence now, which was strange because we had only known each other for an afternoon. Violet eventually spoke.

"I'm only telling you this because it's unlikely I'm going to be here for long enough for it to matter." She paused. "The thing is, I understand what cats say," she said. "When they meow, or when they move their tail in a particular way, or twitch their whiskers, or purr, or any of the other things that cats do, I understand."

"Have you always been able to do this?" I asked, feeling my way.

"I wasn't always as good at it as I am now, and it took me some time to realise I could do it," Violet said. "In the Unfortunate Past I couldn't do it at all."

"The Unfortunate Past?" I asked.

I could hear Tabitha and Greta crawling back towards us and

hoped that Violet wouldn't stop because they were listening.

"She means when she was living …" Tabitha said.

"Actually, we don't talk about the Unfortunate Past," Violet gently interceded. "I prefer to live in the present."

"Ginger ate his dinner after you spoke to him," I said.

"Yes," said Violet, "you need to feed him more fish. He doesn't really like those meaty canned dishes with the sauces. He doesn't like any of those saucy dishes."

"So how do you know that?" I asked. "Tell me about you and cats."

Violet sighed. "It's quite complicated," she said, "and if I tell you, you probably won't believe me anyway."

"Try me," I said and was grateful when she did.

"You see, my family — well, my mother really, Dad's okay — has a particular condition that has made them unpopular. In the past …"

"The Unfortunate Past?" I asked hopefully.

"No, not my particular Unfortunate Past, although some of my family have been through some unfortunate times," said Violet in a sad but matter-of-fact way.

"Unfortunate in what way?" I asked.

"Unfortunate in a burning-at-the-stake, drowning-in-the-river kind of way," piped up Tabitha.

I was conscious of Greta sitting very still beside me, and in the silence that followed I was glad to feel her hand, even though it was sticky. (I dropped it quickly when I remembered it was sticky with banana.)

"Are you saying that you had some family members who were witches?" I asked slowly, the darkness of the attic becoming scarier.

"We prefer the term Creatures of Magic," said Violet.

"Are you a witch?" I asked.

"I am a Creature of Magic, yes," said Violet.

"We're not proper witches. Our main power is the cat thing—" Tabitha interrupted.

"Creatures of Magic," corrected Violet. "And that's enough, Tabitha. We were born with some magical powers. Not as many as Mother, she is a full-blooded Creature of Magic, even though she's currently non-practising, given we are living here. Everyone in the family, except Father who is a completely non-magical person, has some level of skill with magic."

My head was spinning.

"So the cat thing …" I said, trying to start with something I could understand.

"I can understand what cats say and think because I am a Creature of Magic," Violet said.

"Can you do other things, other magic things?" Greta asked.

"Some," said Violet.

"Violet's really good at magic," Tabitha said. "She can do heaps of stuff that Mum doesn't even know about. She's great at cloudwriting, and she's also been working on this magical creature spell ..."

"Hush, Tabitha," said Violet. "I think I can hear someone coming."

5

Doubt, *noun* **when you are not sure you believe someone, or that something is true.**

We all hurried back to our respective bedrooms. I slammed the attic ladder up and leaped into my bed just before Mum came in. "Girls! What was that sound? It's nine-thirty — I thought you were both devastatingly tired? Anna, I heard you leaping into bed. What's going on?"

"Nothing, Mum," Greta said unconvincingly.

I said nothing.

Mum ended up settling Greta down in her and Dad's bed. I crept in to talk to Greta after Mum had gone back downstairs but she had fallen asleep and complained so loudly when I tried to wake her that I gave up.

I couldn't sleep that night.

My mind kept going around in circles. I wasn't sure what the difference was between a witch and a Creature of Magic. They seemed pretty similar. The main thought thudding through my brain was that we had witches living next door. Despite this being a thrilling revelation I couldn't help feeling there was something that Violet and Tabitha were holding back. Those references to the Unfortunate Past had been strange, and the cat thing, while plausible if they were witches, still seemed to be an incomplete explanation – more because of the way Violet continually shut Tabitha up than because it was unbelievable. (What am I writing? The whole thing was unbelievable, but somehow I was inclined to believe them.)

However, as the night wore on and I still couldn't sleep, I started to question whether Violet and Tabitha were just making up an elaborate story. I wanted to believe Violet, but doubts kept creeping in. There was no real evidence to support what she was saying. Yes, Pamela's eating of the flowers had been odd, but that didn't make her a witch. No one had been burned at the stake for eating flowers as far as I was aware, and nothing else in her behaviour had marked her as a witch. Similarly, there had been nothing really magical to date about our time with Violet and Tabitha. Yes, Ginger had eaten his dinner, but magic was not the only possible explanation for this. Ginger seemed to have taken a shine to Violet, but again this didn't necessarily mean Violet was magical. Maybe Violet just had an affinity with animals, cats in particular.

It started to rain quite heavily during the night. I got up to close my window and noticed Pamela in the back corner of their garden, calling out to someone. It was difficult to hear what she was saying because of the rain, but it sounded like she was calling some kind of animal. Her voice had the singsong quality I used when I was calling Ginger in for his dinner.

As I watched, two kittens jumped over the back fence and into Pamela's arms. They were meowing stridently, probably protesting against the rain. As Pamela moved towards the back door I heard her say, "What are you doing, you silly billies, running around in the rain like that? Come inside and get warm. Come on, Brendan, don't scratch Orlando. We'll be inside soon."

A movement in the jacaranda tree next door caught my eye. What looked like a hooded figure was lying flat on a jacaranda branch, looking up towards the Browns' house. I rubbed my eyes and reached over to my bedside table for my glasses, which weren't there. Whatever was in the tree was very still. It was difficult to tell whether it was a hooded figure or a trick of the tree shadows. I watched intently. The branches swayed in the wind. I decided I was wrong. A piece of clothing must be caught in the tree. My discussion with Violet had shifted my imagination into overdrive.

I climbed back into bed. As I tossed and turned I wondered

drowsily how many cats lived with the Browns. Were there as many cats as mice in that house?

❋

I woke up to Greta jumping all over me. "Wake up, Anna, wake UP!" she said, pulling my blanket off me.

"Leave me alone," I groaned, pushing her away.

"Mum said that once you've had your breakfast we're allowed to go next door if we want to. Violet and Tabitha came over this morning and asked whether we could, and Mum said yes as long as we're home for lunch. But it's late, Anna! Unless we go soon we'll hardly have any time there at all. It's already ten o'clock."

"Okay, okay," I said, sliding rather than leaping out of bed.

My brain was fuzzy with tiredness and confused thoughts about witches. But I had to go next door. In the clear light of day, witches and witchcraft seemed a lot less believable than in the darkness of the night. I had questions that I wanted to ask Tabitha and Violet, tough questions about proof. Possibly leading into a lengthy discussion about the importance of honesty between friends. Perhaps leading to an ultimatum about how we couldn't be friends if we couldn't trust each other.

Who was I kidding? I never confronted anyone.

46

I munched on my cereal and composed a list of questions and requests I was going to put to Violet. Nicely. Included in this list was a request for Violet to do some magic, some undeniable magic that would demonstrate beyond doubt the truth of her claims.

It is easy to be indignant and brave in the safety of your own house. Stepping into the dark dustiness of the house next door I felt less confident and was glad Greta was standing beside me. One of the taller taxidermic rodents was being used as a hat stand beside the front door. Children's sunhats were piled high on its hairy head and it shook as I shut the door. I noticed walking past the lounge room that there was a small boy still in his pyjamas having breakfast, with a tabby kitten curled up beside him. The boy looked up at me with eyes that were just like Violet's.

"The girls are upstairs, kittens," Pamela called out from the kitchen. She was wearing an apron with her cat's head brooch pinned to it and was still unpacking. If she was a witch, surely she could use magic to help with this boring job? Witchcraft and housework were words that did not belong together.

"Tell them that they can start unpacking their books onto that bookshelf on the landing," she said. "You can help them if you like."

Violet and Tabitha were upstairs. They had already started unpacking but there were several unopened boxes on the landing.

"Hi," Greta and I said in unison.

"Greetings," said Violet looking up. "You don't believe what I was telling you last night, do you?" It was a question, but barely. I could tell she knew the answer. This was not how I anticipated our meeting would go. I had worked myself up to ask Violet some hard questions, but it seemed I didn't have to. She was asking them for me.

"No," I answered, deciding to follow my internally rehearsed script, even though Violet had taken my part. I would be honest, just as I planned to request Violet to be.

Violet stared at me with her green eyes. "Seeing is believing — you'd like some evidence, wouldn't you?"

Again it was a statement couched as a question.

"Yes," I said.

This was easy. I didn't like confrontations and I felt more comfortable following Violet's lead.

"As you wish," she said. Violet's tone was conversational not aggressive, and I felt that for all her coolness of manner she understood and did not judge me for questioning what she had told me. Or maybe it suited her to show me some proof of magic.

"Follow me," she said, and we followed her to a corridor down from the landing. There were unused rooms full of boxes. My heart started to pound again.

"Come on," Violet said, struggling to lift one of the boxes of books. "Help me carry this up to the landing."

6

Secret, *noun* **something
you keep to yourself.**

"I don't need to tell you that this is top secret," said Violet. "If you tell anyone about this, it could lead to a number of scenarios, all bad. The most obvious is that I'm sure your parents will not let you come over here if they know about us. It could also make things dangerous and unpleasant for our mother, and at its most extreme could result in us having to move again, or maybe even death."

"I won't tell," I promised. Secrecy seemed a fair exchange for the promise of magic.

"This is serious and potentially dangerous," repeated Violet. "I don't know whether it's appropriate for Greta to see this."

"You're not getting rid of me," said Greta. "I'll tell Mum."

Violet rolled her eyes and looked at me. We shared an unspoken moment of acknowledgement of the tedious nature of younger siblings.

"What are you going to do, Vi?" asked Tabitha, slinking up the stairs, surprising me again with the silence of her movement.

"Something I've been planning to do once we moved into this house, something to make things a bit more homelike around here and to help with—" Violet stopped mid-sentence and looked at me thoughtfully, opening one of the boxes stacked on the landing. She pulled out about ten books, flicked through them and put them aside. "Here, Tabitha and Greta, put these books on the shelf will you? We will unpack while we're looking. Anna, you can help me look."

"I want to help look too," Greta said.

"No," said Violet. "Some of these titles are very complicated and the writing can be very difficult to read. I don't think you could manage it."

"If you put the books away, you can climb on that ladder," I suggested. Greta loved to climb.

There was a very old and rickety ladder leaning against the bookshelves. The rungs clung tentatively to a termite-ridden frame. If the rungs didn't collapse under Greta's weight, there was always the risk the bookshelf would fall on top of her. It looked alluring.

"Okay," Greta said, her eyes shining.

"What we're looking for, Anna, is a book from the first

spells series, called *Manipulation of Magical Creatures — Big Creatures for Small Children*. It has a gold cover, is large and will be wrapped in gladwrap," Violet said, passing me a box. "Here, open this one, and pass the checked books over to Greta and Tabitha."

Greta and Tabitha worked smoothly, with Tabitha passing the books to Greta who would then climb up the ladder and place them on the top shelf. The ladder had not collapsed and neither had the bookshelf. "What about the order of the books?" Tabitha asked as we opened another box.

"Don't worry, I'll deal with that later," said Violet. "I want to do it all properly."

"Violet's a neat freak," Tabitha commented to us.

It took about an hour to find the book. Even the ladder was not enough to maintain Greta's interest in the process and she and Tabitha left to play with the mice after about half an hour. Violet and I worked our way through the boxes. Various cats had sauntered up the stairs while we looked, wrapping themselves around Violet before moving on to sit, as cats do, in the most inconvenient spot they could find, mostly on freshly opened boxes of books.

"Why do they bother?" I asked, exasperated, removing a persistent white cat that had sat for the umpteenth time on the pile of books I was sorting through.

"They don't want us to do this," said Violet. "They sense we're doing something Mother wouldn't like and it's their way of slowing us down."

She moved one of two tabby kittens that kept jumping and meowing on an unopened box.

"Move it, Brendan, will you?" she said, annoyed. "Shoo, go outside and play, why don't you? And Orlando, scoot, go practise your talking."

But even uncooperative kittens didn't prevent Violet from finding her sought-after book. She lifted it reverently out of the box and let me hold it. The gladwrap covering the book was soft and warm, and the smell of honey lingered around it. Touching the thick golden letters on the cover thrilled me. I could sense the magic and excitement in its pages and my fingertips tingled the same way my tongue did when I ate fizzy fuzz. When I looked over at Violet I saw my own excitement reflected in her face.

"All right," she said. "Let's do some magic!"

We moved into the small study off the hallway. Empty boxes were stacked haphazardly in the corner. A dead cockroach rested on its back beside a small wooden display cabinet. Some of the smaller taxidermic rodents had been placed inside and their dead gaze was unsettling.

The study had the advantage, as Violet pointed out, of being a long way from the kitchen where her mother was working but the disadvantage of being very hot. There was an old fan on the ceiling that Violet turned on to a low setting. Dust motes moved tiredly through the rearranged air. Violet went to the window, which to my surprise she closed instead of opening further. We sat on the floor in the middle of the room, waiting for what was to come.

My hands trembled as I wiped my forehead. It was dripping with perspiration. My heart was thudding in my chest, and my conscience was twinging. Violet had said that her mother wouldn't want her to do this magic, or whatever it was that she was about to do, and I knew she was doing it for me.

She was thumbing through the pages with a small frown on her face and her bracelet with the bell tinkled with the movement of her wrist. It seemed there was something in particular she was looking for, and I couldn't help looking over Violet's shoulder at the words as she started to alternately mumble and hum.

It was so hot. The drone of the fan, the buzzing of bees outside and the whirr of a distant lawnmower all failed to disturb the heavy heat of the room. I started to feel drowsy and my eyes felt like they were stuck to the words on the page. Before I realised what was happening I had started to read the golden printed

words with Violet. The words were lost to me as soon as they were uttered. My head drooped closer to the book. Perspiration dripped onto the open page as my face went closer and closer to the writing.

The last thing I remember is a perfect drop of perspiration trembling on the open page.

7

Mermaid, *noun* beautiful half-human being,
with the head and trunk of woman and the tail of fish.

"A lovely piece of work," said Pamela Brown.

The golden book was gone and I was resting on Violet's bed with a glass of water in my hand.

"Where's Violet?" I asked, still feeling a bit woozy.

"She's in the bathroom with the mermaid you just summoned," Pamela said briskly. "She's a beautiful creature. Probably not the most appropriate magical creature for this house given the size of the bathroom, and of course illegal, but I suppose we'll just have to make do for now."

I looked at her blankly.

"Mermaid?" I said. "What mermaid?"

"Now, now, Anna," Pamela said. "It was the work of both you and Violet. It needed two voices for an effective summoning, including the voice of a creature without magic, as well as something from your body. I won't ask what she took from you and I don't know how she convinced you to become involved, but I hope it was through fair means not foul. I hope she was honest with you."

Honest? How had I helped to make a mermaid? I didn't remember Violet asking me to help with the spell, and I certainly had no idea what I had contributed as a "creature without magic". Had Violet used me?

My head was reeling and I felt dizzy as I rose from the bed. Pamela steadied me, looking at me with concern. I stood still for a moment, trying to connect mind with body.

"Where is the bathroom?" I asked.

"She's in the upstairs bathroom. Now take it slowly," Pamela said gently. "And here, take these." She handed me a pair of large earmuffs. "A mermaid's song can be dangerous; in the worst instance, fatal," she said, smiling in a way that made fatality sound inconvenient rather than tragic. "It's best to be prepared. I don't really know how I would explain it to your mother if you were to become comatosed or mad for that matter. And tell Violet to come and see me after you've spoken to her."

I raced to the bathroom. I heard a sound like choir music and, mindful of Pamela's warning, I put on my earmuffs. They were too big for me and as I ran they bounced up and down over my ears, and the dim sounds that filtered through flickered on and off like faulty radio reception. I held them firmly over my ears as I opened the bathroom door. Violet was there, and resting in the bathtub, with a sulky expression on her beautiful face, was a mermaid. From where I stood in the doorway you couldn't really tell she was a mermaid. Her thick, muscular tail was obscured by the bathtub rim but when I moved closer I saw it swishing around in the water. She wasn't as big as I thought she would be. She was the size of a small grown-up and despite it being a bit of a squash she did fit in the bath. She was brushing her long, golden wavy hair and her eyes were bright blue.

Violet was talking but I couldn't hear through my earmuffs. Whatever she was saying, the mermaid wasn't happy about it. She flicked her tail and hair about in an angry way. The mermaid pointed out the window and shouted. The bathroom looked out onto the building site next door to the Browns, where builders were hard at work. They showed no interest in us even though the mermaid was obviously interested in them. Violet talked some more, making me wish I could lip-read, and she too pointed out at the builders and then to me. She pointed at the mermaid, then at her cat brooch and then swiped two fingers across her throat in a gesture of finality. The mermaid nodded in a sulky kind of way and Violet grinned at me and gave me the thumbs up. She motioned for me to remove my earmuffs.

"Anna," she said, "meet Charlene. Charlene, this is Anna. She helped to summon you."

Charlene took my hand. It felt very cold and she smelled of the sea. She then gave a deep bow and theatrically flung out her arms. "Devastated to meet you, oh Creature of Magic, who has summoned me from the watery depths to hear my thrilling song. Oh, were I still there how I would enjoy singing my terrible song and luring you to your death among the waves, to slip through the water together, death sweet death—"

"I think that's enough of the doom and gloom, Charlene," Violet said briskly. "I gather you're not happy about being here in our bathroom, but you are going to have to make do. Look at it as an adventure."

"Adventure?" shrieked Charlene. "The open sea is an adventure. This is a prison, this tiny room with no one to lure to their death in the watery depths. Why have you summoned me, sorcerer? Have I drowned one of your relatives for you to desire to punish me so?"

"Not that I am aware of, Charlene," said Violet. "I agree, it would be difficult for anyone to drown in this bath, thankfully, but unlike you I don't see that as a bad thing. Maybe you could get to know us and perhaps you would find that it was more fun talking to us than luring us to our deaths."

"Yes," I said, feeling it was time for me to assert myself. "Really, talking to us would be a lot more fun than killing us."

Charlene snorted. It sounded like water being sucked down an ocean bogey hole. She looked at me with scorn.

"Talk?" she made the word sound like it had three syllables rather than one. "I don't think so, not if the conversation I've heard so far is anything to go by. Fun? I am a creature of tragedy and despair! I am the heroine in the tragedy that is my life, not some minor character in the third-rate children's comedy that might be yours. My language is the language of love and the madness of desire, of men who would drown just to hear my song. Show me the sailors, I say. Let me sing!"

During this tirade Charlene had hoisted herself onto the ledge of the bath so her head was level with the open window. With another wriggle her head was out the window and with her long golden hair and top half dangling she began to sing at the builders.

Violet lunged over and put my earphones back on my ears just as the glorious sound of Charlene's voice started. We watched in silence as the builders next door pointed and gestured at Charlene, slowly sinking to their knees. One by one they fell to the ground.

Violet was madly pulling Charlene away from the window,

and as I went to help her I caught a glimpse of a man in the Browns' backyard. He was looking up at Charlene with a rapt expression on his face. As we pulled the mermaid back down into the bath he too sank to his knees and passed out. Violet's mouth was moving in an angry way and I saw her point with a vehement finger to her cat-shaped brooch. Charlene stopped singing and dropped back down into the bath, rearranging her hair so it covered her face. She sat still and quiet. Violet motioned to me to take my earmuffs off and as I did something occurred to me.

"How come Charlene's song didn't hurt you?" I asked. "You weren't wearing earmuffs."

"No," said Violet. "I'm a Creature of Magic. Charlene's song can't hurt me. Do you believe me now, Anna?" she asked seriously.

I nodded. As I helped her close the window I glanced at the comatose man in their back garden. Violet did too and she sighed. "Father is not a Creature of Magic," she said. "He is going to be so angry!"

8

Apothecary, *noun* **an old-fashioned word for doctor or chemist.**

Pamela was back in the kitchen unpacking cups and plates. Unwrapping crockery from newspaper seemed a world away from mermaids in bathtubs, and as I watched her I had a feeling that became very familiar over the summer holidays. It was disbelief at how the Browns could be so ordinary and so extraordinary at the same time.

"Mother," Violet said tentatively, fiddling with her cat brooch. "There's been a few problems with the mermaid. She's been up to a bit of mischief."

"I can't say I'm surprised," said Pamela, continuing with her unwrapping, the bell on her leather bracelet ringing softly with the motion. "Really, Violet, I am a bit cross with you for summoning her, and please call me Mum! You know we are all trying to make a fresh start in the non-magical community for Dad. Having a mermaid upstairs is not normal practice around here, as I'm sure you out of everyone would realise. It wouldn't even be standard in magical communities, though of course they would be more understanding. This could have serious consequences, Violet. It's illegal, and while you might be able to get away with it because you're a minor ..."

Pamela looked at Violet with a funny expression on her face. In a different tone she added, "It is a very difficult spell, Violet. I'm surprised you had the power to do it at your age. You really are talented, darling." Pamela seemed to remember she was angry. She reverted to her angry voice and added, "It's unfair you doing something like this when you know I'm not allowed to do any magic to reverse it. We spoke about this when we moved. Dad and I made it very clear what the rules were, and they're not just our rules they are the LAW and who knows where the closest apothecary is!"

I knew the word but it took me a moment to remember it meant chemist. Pamela glared at Violet but it wasn't a seriously angry glare. You could tell she was more exasperated than angry.

"What's she done in her first half-hour of life here anyway?"

"Umm, she insisted on singing out of the window and—"

"What?" shrieked Pamela. "I told you to keep her secure. Violet, an open window is not secure. How many people has she knocked out?"

"Four so far," said Violet. "There were three builders on the building site next door."

"Oh no," groaned Pamela. "This is not what I need right now, Violet, with all this unpacking and your little brothers running around goodness knows where. Who is the fourth person?"

"Um, well, I think Father heard her," said Violet, following her mother out of the kitchen into the backyard. "But I think that's it. I don't think you can see the bathroom window from anywhere except our backyard and the building site. If anyone else heard her, they probably wouldn't link her voice to our house."

"Lucky for us," said Pamela, grimly. "If anyone else overheard her they will just have to sleep it out. Run upstairs and get that book you used to summon Charlene and bring it down here. And that's another thing, what were you thinking bringing that book here? You know it's not allowed. It is ILLEGAL, Violet." She paused for a moment and said quickly, "But seeing as it's here we may as well use it. There should be something in it about assisted recovery of mermaid victims. They're lucky, those builders. If they'd been out at sea and heard Charlene, they would have been dragged under water and drowned. Probably the worst that can happen to them here is a bit of a headache from hitting their heads on the concrete slab."

I followed Violet up the stairs. She grabbed the golden book that was still lying open on the floor of the study. "Greta!" I suddenly thought. "Violet, where's Greta?"

"I don't know," said Violet. "She went off with Tabitha. I think they were going to make a mouse house in the backyard. Tabitha probably fell asleep in the sun."

I looked out the window and saw Greta's blond head near the strawberry patch. My relief was short-lived – Greta was very, very still.

"Great," I said. "I think Greta must have heard Charlene as well. Do you think your Mum could fix her up before she gets to the builders? Mum is going to be calling out for us soon and if we don't come back, she'll probably come over here looking for us."

"If you wish," said Violet. "I'll ask Mum to do Greta first."

Greta looked at me blankly when I had told her we were going home for lunch. I wasn't sure whether it was her own name or where her home was that she had forgotten, but either way I didn't want Mum getting wind that anything was up.

Luckily, Mum was on the phone and I managed to eat a sandwich and half of Greta's before making an escape upstairs. Greta was too groggy to eat, but Mum didn't notice.

"I think we might play upstairs for a while," I told Mum,

taking Greta by the hand and half dragging her with me. Pamela had said it would take a few hours for Greta to recover completely, and that in the meantime she probably wouldn't remember much that had happened recently, or indeed anything much at all.

"Beautiful woman, beautiful song," Greta muttered as I pulled her up the stairs.

"What's she saying?" Mum asked.

"Just some music we were listening to next door," I said, going into the study. "Greta really enjoyed it."

I had another reason for going upstairs. If you leaned right out of the study window, you could see the building site. I grabbed Dad's bird-watching binoculars. I wanted to see how Pamela was getting on with the revival of the builders. I watched them walk over John Brown's prostrate body on the way to the building site. As I watched they gave a quick glance around. Violet waved to me and I saw Pamela shrug as they climbed onto the site. The builders were lying close together with happy smiles on their faces. One of them looked familiar, and through his slightly open mouth I saw the glint of a gold tooth. The workmen looked like they were dreaming wonderful dreams, and as I glanced across at Greta I saw the same goofy smile on her sleeping face.

When I looked out the window again I was surprised to see that the sky had clouded over and that rain was falling heavily.

It was difficult to see what Pamela and Violet were doing over at the building site and I guessed that this might be the reason for the rain. Within a couple of minutes, the rain stopped and the sun was shining again. I saw the builders waking up and stretching and Pamela pointing over to her house. Gingerly, the builders, Pamela and Violet climbed down off the site.

I could see John Brown still lying on the ground and hoped that the builders wouldn't notice him. The same thought must have occurred to Violet and, as I watched, John Brown disappeared. He started off by fading, then turned into a shadow and then disappeared completely. I was impressed. As Violet walked up the back stairs she looked up at me and waved, confident that I had seen her magic. I waved back.

Violet had convinced me she could do magic. But I couldn't help thinking about the part I'd unwittingly played in the spell to summon Charlene. It bothered me that Violet hadn't been honest with me. Why hadn't she told me what she was doing and asked me to help? I would have said yes. Looking at Greta lying comatose beside me, I realised that despite magic being fun, it was also dangerous. And not being able to trust Violet made it more dangerous still.

9

Trust, *noun* reliance on the integrity, strength,
ability, surety, etc. of person or thing; confidence.

"Father was so angry," Violet said. "But Mother was
possibly angrier."

It was the next day. Violet had come over to our house
to return Mum's vase and had stayed for most of the morning.
We were upstairs in my bedroom. Violet was drawing and I was
idly reading through the "t" words in the dictionary. Violet filled
me in on the rest of the events of "Charlene Day", as we named it.

"You wouldn't believe it. Charlene managed to escape from
the bathroom while Mother was giving the builders, including
Roger, a cup of tea. Mother told them she saw them collapsing
on the site and thought they must have all suffered simultaneous
heat stroke."

"Who's Roger?" I asked.

"Oh, he's just part of the Bureau. He's supposed to keep
an eye on us. Uncle Roger pops up everywhere," Violet said

vaguely. "Anyway, Charlene managed to wriggle over to Father's harp and was playing it when Mother woke him and he hit the roof. No one is allowed to touch his harp. He may find it difficult to adjust to Charlene living with us," she pondered. "It's unfortunate she covets his harp. And all that talk about luring people to their death in the ocean, well, it's not going to make you popular, is it?"

"No," I said. "Neither is making people unconscious by singing to them. Or using people to summon a mermaid without explaining what you are doing." It slipped out, my comment about the mermaid. I didn't like criticising my friends.

Violet giggled and then stopped when she saw I was serious. "You're upset that I didn't tell you the spell would draw you in and that I needed you to perspire on the page?"

"Seeing as you're asking, yes, I am," I admitted with some anxiety. "Just a bit. You could have asked."

"But what if you had said no?" Violet said. "I'd be up a creek without a paddle."

"Maybe," I said.

"I couldn't take that risk," Violet said. "I need to have Charlene here."

I realised something about Violet then. She had different priorities to me, and despite the fun we had together I didn't understand her. I didn't trust her. To talk more about it would have meant a confrontation so I left it.

Violet sighed. "Mother is upset with me too."

I looked at Violet. She didn't seem upset herself.

"Did you get into trouble?" I asked, wondering what happened when witch children got into trouble.

"Not really," said Violet. "They think I did it to get out of having a bath, which I didn't, but is definitely a bonus."

"Don't you like baths?" I asked.

"I absolutely detest baths," Violet said solemnly, giving a shiver of disgust. "There is a shower in the bathroom downstairs that we use, but a shower is, you know, less wet. You can dodge a lot of water in the shower. It's difficult to avoid getting wet in a bath. And if that's what Mother and Father think, fine. Keeps them from thinking about other reasons I might want Charlene around."

"Other reasons being ...?" I looked at Violet, who continued talking as though I hadn't spoken.

"Mother and Father are so happy I'm at home that they don't really get cross with me. It drives Tabitha crazy. And they didn't say anything much about the fact that I had brought the spell book with us in the first place, which is a big no-no. We could get into a lot of trouble for having that book — it's illegal to have it here." Violet paused and smiled at this point. "Look, it's complicated, but Mother likes that I'm good at magic, and I suppose it's a bit like you need to practise the piano when you're learning to play. Although magic is a piano Father would prefer us not to play."

My face must have shown that she had lost me. Violet tried to explain. "I mean that while we are living here," she pulled a face, "and I'm not supposed to do magic, Mother's a bit worried that I'll lose what I've learned if I don't practise occasionally. I think Mother guesses the summoning wasn't all about bath avoidance."

"Summoning?" I asked.

"Summoning of Charlene," she said. "I think Mother suspects I did it to protect our family, but we don't talk about stuff like that. We don't talk about some of the bad things that have happened in our family. I don't know why, we just don't."

"What are you protecting your family from?" I asked. Surely Violet's magic made her invincible?

"Some people don't like magical things," said Violet. "And they are not happy to just leave it as not liking. There are people who are actually trying to get rid of magic and Creatures of Magic, or at least send us back to our own land. And it's complicated because Father isn't at all magical and he needs to live somewhere where he can do his job, which is music. And while we are living here Mother isn't allowed to do magic. It's one of the rules of living in the non-magical world. But they want to be fair about where they live. We've tried living in Mother's world, which Father was keen about at first, but I think he got sick of feeling different all the time because he can't do magic. And Tabitha felt a bit like that as well. School was challenging for her because she finds magic difficult."

Violet's fake grown-up tone at this point made me roll my eyes. School being challenging is the kind of thing my mother would say. And all this talk of "mother" and "father". It sounded so formal and fake, like they were people she didn't know very well. I didn't interrupt though — even Violet's annoying tone didn't stop me from wanting to hear more.

Oblivious, Violet continued. "And Tabitha's scared of the dark. She used to be teased a lot. Being nocturnal and scared of the dark made life in the Other Place tricky. And Mother has always enjoyed the non-magical world. She finds it all very exciting and doesn't worry about being different, so we thought on balance it would be best for everyone if we moved back. Best for everyone except me and my big brother Tom," she added as an afterthought.

It was the most I had heard Violet say in one go.

"Don't you want to live here, Violet?" I asked.

"I'd prefer not to talk about how I feel about it," she said. "There's no point. We're here now, and we have to deal with the danger as it comes."

"Danger?" I asked. It sounded a bit dramatic.

"Look, Anna, you probably wouldn't understand. I mean, there's the Bureau, but they're not always watching the right people," she said. A frown had appeared on her forehead.

My head was spinning.

"Who is this Bureau?" I asked.

"The Bureau for the Protection of Creatures of Magic," said Violet, wearily. "Unfortunately, they seem to watch us more to make sure we're not breaking any laws by doing magic, rather than to protect us from the Inquisitors."

"Is the Bureau magic?" I asked. "And who are the Inquisitors?"

"No, the Bureau's not magic, they're like you. They are part of your government. No one is supposed to know about them though. They're a top-secret department."

"And what about the Inquisitors?" I asked.

"I don't want to talk about them," she said. "I won't talk about them." Her voice trembled a bit and she looked away.

"Why did you tell me about you being magic?" I asked. "I mean if it was a secret and everything."

Violet was silent.

Over the last couple of days I had learned about Violet's silence. It meant that she was thinking and you had to wait. She chose her words carefully and didn't blab on like I sometimes did. The problem though was the more silent she was, the more likely I was to blab on and I sometimes regretted the things I blabbed.

Violet was watching me as I thought. "I knew I could trust you," she said. "I knew that we would be friends and that you would help me."

"How did you know?" I asked, feeling warm and fuzzy inside. "Was it through magic?"

"Kind of," she said. "Instinct is a kind of magic."

I looked at her curiously. "Why are your mum and dad so glad to have you home?" I asked. "Where have you been?"

Violet was silent. It was no longer a thinking kind of silence but an I-don't-really-want-to-talk-about-it kind of silence.

I didn't ask any more questions. Violet had shared enough with me for the time being. And I knew she trusted me and that she would tell me more when she was ready.

But could I trust her?

Transmogrify, *verb* **to transform
in a magical or surprising manner.**

Violet's four-year-old twin brothers, Brendan and Orlando, were a mystery. Sometimes they were everywhere underfoot, sometimes they seemed to disappear. I overheard Mum talking to Dad about them.

"I don't know what she does with the little boys," she said. "I've seen them once or twice, but she doesn't take them out much. And one of them never speaks. Pamela seems to spend more time playing with the kittens than the children."

I found out more about Brendan and Orlando by accident. One night it was really hot and I had trouble sleeping. I opened my window right up to get some cool air into the bedroom and I noticed Pamela out in the backyard doing a spot of midnight gardening. This was not unusual. Pamela often talked about her enjoyment of "gardening by moonlight". She explained that it was cooler and also a time when she could give the garden her complete attention without having to worry about the children.

Personally, I felt Pamela's midnight gardening had less to do with her children and more to do with her unusual gardening methods, which she preferred to indulge in without anyone watching. I had seen her singing to her strawberries, and the song had inspired the strawberries to grow more than any natural method I had seen. When she sang you could see the strawberries pushing out white flowers, like a chorus in response, and swelling like red balloons being filled with gas.

This particular night however, she wasn't singing. She was calling some of their cats, the numbers of which I had never established. It was difficult to tell which cats belonged to the Browns, as most of the cats in the suburb seemed to hang out there at least some of the time.

I saw the two tabby kittens that often seemed to be out late, playing around Pamela's feet. One leaped into Pamela's arms. Then something happened that woke me right up. I reached for Dad's bird-watching binoculars, which I had decided to keep by my bed in case any other exciting events happened next door. The kitten at Pamela's feet had disappeared and in its place was one of Violet's younger brothers, Brendan. He was rubbing against his mother's legs in a cat-like way and Pamela waved her free arm in a magical gesture. The remaining kitten jumped free

and began to grow. Its two front paws shrank into themselves and then elongated out again like a stalk growing out of a plant. Little fingers emerged from hands that were being sculpted at the end of the arms and at the same time the tabby fur on the cat's body shrunk back beneath the skin that started to glow pinkish and humanlike. His pyjamas became visible and flattened onto his skin as the tabby fur receded. It was Orlando, Violet's little brother. He meowed. At one stage Orlando looked like a boy with a hairy cat's face until his whiskers and fur retreated and his little boy face emerged. Pamela led the two yawning boys inside.

As I lay back down in bed I wondered whether Violet could morph into a cat like her brothers. I would have to ask her tomorrow.

🌸

I didn't think I'd ever get to sleep. But I did. I slept briefly and then the strangeness of the night continued. I had kicked my sheets off in my sleep and mozzies had feasted on my uncovered legs. The itching drove me crazy. I indulged in a good bit of scratching, which unfortunately wasn't very satisfying and just made me itchier, which was always the case with itching.

I scratched so much that one of the bites started bleeding. I knew I needed a bandaid. They were kept in the medicine cabinet in the hall cupboard, but I hated going downstairs in the dark by myself. I knew where Tabitha was coming from with this. I tried to wake Greta but she muttered and carried on so much I gave up and braved the dark stairs on my own.

I found the medicine box easily, but while I was bandaiding myself I heard a strange snuffling sound coming from outside the front gate. Because the front of our house was one big room, from the dining table you could see straight out onto the street. And what I saw outside our fence distracted me from my irritatingly itchy legs.

John Brown was standing on the street holding a large animal on a leash. It looked like a cross between a small horse and a large dog, but its claws were definitely not hoofs and even in the dim glow of the streetlight you could see its big teeth. It was very hairy. I crept to the front window and looked out.

John Brown was too distracted to see me. He was swearing under his breath, and it took me a moment to realise what he was doing. The animal appeared to have done a poo in the small nature strip around the crepe myrtle tree outside our house. It was a small tree, but unfortunately the animal's poo was in keeping with its magnificent size. Like a responsible pet owner, John Brown was trying to collect the poo but the plastic bag he had brought was too small for that purpose. With a sigh he tethered the animal inside the front gate and went inside the house to find another plastic bag.

I gently opened our front door and took a stool outside to climb up on and then looked over our side fence into the Browns' front yard.

The animal heard me and looked up. It had a long face not unlike a horse, but its teeth, which were more like fangs, hung out on either side of its slack mouth, with a long floppy dog's tongue lolling between them. These fangs should have made it scary, particularly given its size, but it really looked more goofy than scary. It didn't look stupid though. Its large brown eyes seemed to mirror the curiosity I felt about it.

When I heard John Brown rustling towards their front door with what sounded like any number of plastic bags I ducked off the stool and quietly moved back inside the house, timing my shutting of the front door with the creaking of their front gate. I felt that John Brown would not want me to know about the dog that did not quite seem to be a dog. If he wanted people to see it, he would be walking it in broad daylight rather than the middle of night. I had a lot of questions for Violet.

11

Spy, *verb* to secretly watch other people or things
to work out important information.

Unfortunately, I didn't get the opportunity to ask Violet about her brothers or the dog-like creature the next day. Mum had arranged to take me, Greta, Violet and Tabitha into the city to see Santa Claus, something that Greta and I were definitely over. I felt that sitting on Santa Claus's knee at my age was pretty demeaning. Mum had a series of photos of me with Santa where I was crying in the beginning, looking really excited from about ages four to seven and bored from then on.

To my surprise both Violet and Tabitha thought that going to see Santa Claus sounded like a lot of fun, so we were all going together the day before Christmas Eve.

It was a hot day. There was no air conditioning on the train we caught into the city, and even the vinyl seats were warm. Greta's face was red and sweaty and mine felt the same.

"Lovely hot day, isn't it? Perfect day for petitions to St Nicholas?" Tabitha enthused.

"It's hot, but I wouldn't describe it as lovely," I said. Tabitha and Violet looked cool and fresh and sleek. The hot weather agreed with them but they looked tired. Violet yawned. I could imagine her happily curling up on the warm seat and going to sleep.

I looked around the train. There was a man wearing shorts and shiny leather boots, reading a newspaper a few seats behind us. He had a toolkit and hard hat beside him. The newspaper rustled as he turned the pages and Tabitha looked around. I saw the man wink at her over the top of the newspaper, and as he grinned I saw the glint of a gold tooth.

Tabitha looked at him curiously for a moment and then exclaimed, "Roger! Uncle Roger — what are you doing here?"

Violet nudged her. "His job, Tabs. He's doing his job, which is supposed to be undercover." She whispered the word "undercover".

"Best we don't talk, love. You know, on duty and all that. Probably drop by Chrissie Day with Olivia," he said quietly.

At the sound of their voices Mum looked up from her book and turned around. "Hello," she said. "I'm Dorothy. We live next door to Violet and Tabitha. Are you a friend of the girls?"

"No," Violet said quickly.

"Know these little girls?" said Roger, looking surprised at the question. "No, I don't believe I do. Just minding my own business here, reading my newspaper, as people do, on my way to work." He turned the page of the newspaper with a great deal of rustling and then hid behind it.

Mum looked from newspaper-reading man to Violet and Tabitha. "We'll let you get back to your newspaper then," she said, puzzled. "Girls, we might move downstairs, we're getting close to the city now." She took Greta's and Tabitha's hands and we moved downstairs.

We were nowhere near the city.

"Did that man just start talking to you?" she asked Tabitha. "What was he saying?"

Tabitha looked at Violet. "Roger didn't say anything," Tabitha said.

Violet groaned.

"I thought you said you didn't know him?" Mum asked.

Violet took over. "We don't know him. Tabs thought he looked like someone we know called Roger, but when she spoke to him she realised he wasn't."

"Yes," said Tabitha, unconvincingly. "That's right."

I wasn't interested in Roger. I knew he worked for the Bureau.

I wanted to talk about what I had seen the previous night.

But I didn't get a chance once we were in Santa's cave either. It was absolutely crazy in there with babies crying, parents trying to comfort them and children whinging about the length of a line that was definitely longer than the average toddler's capacity to wait.

I felt a bit daggy being there with all the little kids but Violet and Tabitha were really excited. It was as if they had never seen anything like it before and their excitement was contagious. They marvelled at the merry-go-round. "Look, Vi, horses that have been turned into plastic and impaled!" Tabitha said, wide-eyed. The lucky dip left Tabitha almost speechless. "Plastic toys," she whispered, opening up the bag, "wrapped in plastic!"

"You don't have plastic toys?" Mum asked.

"Not where we come from," Tabitha said, holding her plastic toy close.

I could tell Mum approved.

Violet, despite being less effusive, was no less impressed. I could tell she was trying not to show it. She wasn't saying much but her eyes were shining and when Mum, sensing the Brown girls' excitement, suggested we had a ride on the merry-go-round I jumped at the opportunity to have a relatively private conversation with Violet. It was useless though. Violet was too taken with the merry-go-round and the noise of all the surrounding children made any conversation difficult to hear. It wasn't until we were actually inside with Santa that I thought of a way to talk to Violet about the animal I had seen, even with Mum and Greta and Tabitha being around.

Greta and I had our usual photograph taken with Santa, which made Mum emotional for some reason.

"You're getting so grown up," she said, dabbing her eyes with a tissue. "It seems like yesterday you were just babies, sitting there on Santa's knee."

Santa Claus coughed politely. "Is there anything you young ladies would like in particular for Christmas?" he asked.

"Well," I said, "since you ask, there is something."

"Yes, little girl?" asked Santa, encouragingly.

"I'd like a dog," I said.

Mum groaned and stopped dabbing her eyes.

"Well, not a dog-dog, more a dog that looks like a horse with big teeth and that likes to walk at night," I said.

Mum rolled her eyes.

"I think we might be out of those," Santa said tiredly. "What about a dolly?"

Greta, Tabitha and I all rolled our eyes. Violet just looked at me, frowning.

"Come on, Greta," I said, trying to take her hand. "I think our turn has finished."

"Speak for yourself, Anna," she said unfazed and then addressed Santa. "Don't worry, I'll be quick. An iPad, I'd like an iPad."

"Mmm," said Santa.

"And what about you children?" he turned to Violet and Tabitha.

"Well," said Tabitha, excited. "I'd like an i-pid, an umbrella made out of plastic, a game in a small box that you poke with a stick to make things move, and some music in a box that you sing along to."

"She means an iPad and a DS," said Greta, helpfully, "and a karaoke set."

"I think that's enough for one little girl, more than enough," said Santa, looking at his watch. He turned to Violet.

Tabitha jumped off his lap. "Thanks," she said. "Any one of those things would be great."

"And what about you?" Santa looked at Violet who moved no closer.

"Ummm, I don't think I want anything you can help me with," she said.

"Try me, *ho ho ho*," Santa boomed, and then looked a bit

scared. I guessed he was preparing himself for one of those tricky requests, like divorced parents getting back together, or sick people getting better, fathers home from war, that kind of stuff.

"I'd like my brother to come home for Christmas," Violet said. "And a loom would be nice."

"I'll do my best," said Santa. "We don't get a lot of requests for looms. I'll have to check what the elves have in stock."

Violet clammed up when I asked her about her brother and why she would want a loom. It was a quiet trip home, although I managed to get a bit of information from the talkative Tabitha. Mum asked me in an exasperated kind of way why I would want a dog, given the amount of discussion we'd already had about it, and the agreement she thought she had from me that a dog was not a good idea at this point in time. Surprisingly, or not so surprisingly, had I thought about it, Tabitha and Violet supported Mum.

"Why would you want a dog?" asked Tabitha, puzzled. "They are so slobbery and always want to play with you and poo everywhere. Cats are so much more fun, and Ginger is such a lovely cat too."

"There are dogs that are not really all that dog-like," I said. "In fact I have seen some dogs that look more like small horses."

"Oh, you mean like Wocky?" said Tabitha. "Dad's dog that

isn't a dog? Have you seen him? I thought he was supposed to a secret ..."

"Which generally means something you keep silent about," said Violet, giving Tabitha a very dirty look.

"Oh, does your father have a dog?" asked Mum. "I haven't seen or heard it. Does he ever take it out for a walk?"

"Only at night," said Tabitha, ignoring Violet. "Wocky's nocturnal."

"Nocturnal?" asked Mum. "Like an owl?"

"He looks more like a horse than a dog and he doesn't have wings, so no, not much like an owl," explained Tabitha.

"Tabitha has a very active imagination," Violet said to Mum in the grown-up manner I found so annoying.

"Are you saying your father doesn't have a dog?" asked Mum, completely bewildered.

Violet said firmly, "I can honestly say he does not have a dog."

As she spoke her hair, which was out of its usual ponytail, fell back and Mum caught a glimpse of Violet's cat brooch.

"How pretty!" Mum exclaimed. "That really is lovely; was that a present from your parents?"

"In a manner of speaking," Violet said, stiffening and rearranging her hair so it covered the brooch.

The conversation diverted from nocturnal dog-like horses

and brooches to iPads, the practicality of looms and Christmas in general. Tabitha happily chattered to Mum about what her family liked to do for Christmas (open presents, eat lots of seafood and sleep) and Mum didn't notice that Violet was silent for the rest of the trip home.

I thought about the dog that wasn't a dog and the little boys being kittens. And the Inquisitors — who were they? If Violet knew about them, Tabitha would know about them. I knew that if I wanted to find out more, my best chance would be to talk to Tabitha. Alone.

12

Candour, *noun* the quality of being honest and telling
the truth, even about a difficult or embarrassing subject.

Later that day, I saw Tabitha go out into the backyard
and watched her aimlessly pushing the swing. Violet was
nowhere in sight and Mum and Greta were down at the
shops getting groceries. I ducked downstairs and shimmied up
the tree that looked over the Browns' backyard.

"Pssssst, Tabitha," I whispered.

She looked up straightaway. Her hearing, like everyone's in
the Brown family (except John Brown), was acute.

"If you're looking for Violet, she's out with Mum," she said.

"No, it was you I was looking for," I said, and felt bad as
I watched Tabitha's face brighten. She wasn't used to be being
the one who was sought out, and I thought how many times
Violet and I had shut the door on her when she tried to join in
whatever we were doing. Admittedly, she'd had Greta to play
with and we had excluded Greta as well, but Greta deserved to

be excluded because she was annoying. However, even annoying sisters deserved Christmas presents, and this was going to be my excuse for getting Tabitha over.

"Um, do you want to come to our house? I need to get Greta something for her mice, Sugar, Marmalade and Fuzzy, for Christmas and thought you might help me choose something from the pet shop website."

"Sure," Tabitha said. "That sounds fun. I'll just tell Dad where I'm going."

She yelled out, "Dad, I'm going over to Anna's."

John Brown didn't answer, probably because he hadn't heard. This didn't seem to worry Tabitha, who with her usual grace leaped over the fence into our backyard.

We poured over the pet shop website, with Tabitha choosing an array of plastic toys for Sugar and friends, with a focus on entrapment. Mum had promised she would pick up the presents I had chosen tomorrow, as long as I let her know exactly what they were. Tabitha continued to highlight different things on the website. Like Greta she loved technology, and as they didn't seem too big on it next door she enjoyed mucking around on our computer.

"So, Tabitha," I said, "I had a couple of questions about Wocky."

"Mm," Tabitha said, looking at some cute fishy kitten bowls. "These would be great presents for Orlando and Brendan. Do you think your mum could get them for me tomorrow when she's at the pet shop?"

"Yeah, sure," I said. "But getting back to Wocky ..."

"Wocky's real name is Rocky," Tabitha explained. "I couldn't say Rocky when we first got him and I used to call him 'Wocky' and the name stuck. He is Dad's pet," Tabitha clarified. "Wocky is not a *dog*," she spat the word dog out like a cat with a furball, "but he is the closest Mum could find to a dog in the Other Place. Dad often felt homesick and he used to tell us bedtime stories about the dog that he'd had as a pet when he was a boy. Mum gave him a taxidermic dog one year for Christmas but—"

"He didn't like it?" I interrupted.

Tabitha looked at me, surprised. "How did you know?" she asked. "No, he didn't like it. He was really angry about it and made Mum take it back, which upset her. She had gone to heaps of trouble to find it. There are no living dogs in the Other Place, so dead ones weren't that easy to come by either."

"So if he's not a dog, what is Wocky?" I asked.

"I'm not sure exactly what Wocky is to be honest," Tabitha said. "I think there is a name for what he is, but I can't remember it. He's an animal, and he is kind of like I imagine a dog to be. He likes balls — more to eat than to fetch really — and he likes to lick things and needs to be taken for a walk, but he is different to a dog in that he is nocturnal and very smart."

I was about to contradict Tabitha but didn't want to interrupt this flow of very interesting information. She was a human, or not quite human, tap.

"He understands human speech quite well, but he doesn't speak it. He's unusual even in the Other Place, you know, endangered almost. It was difficult getting him here from the Other Place, that's for sure. Mum wanted to leave Wocky behind and sell him to a breeding program, but Dad got quite emotional and insisted on bringing him. I know that Mum and Dad want him kept a secret ..." She stopped. "Whoops," she said cheerfully. "Glad Violet's not here."

I was too.

"Can I see him?" I asked. I felt a bit disloyal to Violet doing this, but knew I could keep a secret, unlike Tabitha. And I was sure Tabitha would tell Violet about today anyway because she told everyone everything. So it wasn't like I was really going behind Violet's back.

"I suppose so, now that you know about him," said Tabitha. "It's daylight so he'll be asleep. But you need to promise me you won't talk about him to your parents or friends."

I promised.

We went downstairs and climbed over the fence into the Browns' backyard. The cellar under the house was our destination. It was dark and creepy and I remembered that Tabitha was scared of the dark, just like me. I stood very close to her — we didn't have to pretend to each other that we were braver than we were.

"Be quiet," she whispered. "He doesn't like being woken up. It can make him grumpy."

She led the way into the cellar. I heard Wocky before I saw him. He was snoring at a volume you would expect from a dog the size of a horse and dribbling a bit out of the side of his mouth, which close up was very large. Sharp, yellow fangs poked through his slack mouth and his feet were bigger than my father's. The nails on them were long and tapered to a point like claws.

"Cute, isn't he?" said Tabitha.

Cute wasn't the word I would have used to describe Wocky, but there was something appealing about him. Despite his sharp claws and fangs he was not threatening in his slumbering, dribbling state. Tabitha took my hand and we crept out.

"Thanks, Tabitha," I said.

"That's okay," she said, smiling. "No problem. Any questions, I'm the one to ask."

She was right. I thought of all the other things Violet had mentioned but not explained.

"Well, now that you mention it there was something – Uncle Roger on the train. I know he works for the Bureau, but why do you call him 'uncle'? Is he your mum's brother or something?"

"Oh no, he's not related." Tabitha laughed. "There's nothing magical about Roger, even though his wife is like us."

"And what about the Inquisitors, who are they?"

Tabitha stopped laughing. "The Inquisitoriers are bad," she said slowly, mispronouncing the word. "And some of them are evil, like Arthur—"

The sound of Violet's voice from the kitchen cut our conversation short.

"Come on, Tabitha. Mother says it's time for a shower."

Violet hadn't seen me. Tabitha screwed up her nose at the thought of a shower.

"Remember, it's a secret," she whispered as she went inside. "And really, you don't want to know about the Inquisitoriers."

13

Swing. *noun* a seat attached to a rope or chain that moves
in an arc; something that is fun to ride on and that children
request their parents to push them on in parks.

It was Christmas Eve and Violet and I were swinging on the
two swings the Browns had rigged up in their backyard, and
eating Pamela's apple-sized strawberries.

There were two big jacaranda trees with branches that
reached across the backyard at the same angle but at first there
had only been one swing. Pamela had noticed Violet and I taking
turns, and asked whether it would be more fun if we could
swing together on separate swings. The next time I was over at
the Browns' there was another swing on the neighbouring tree.
The branches of the two trees had suddenly become completely
symmetrical and the second swing swung at the same angle as the
first. You could swing in complete unison and talk at the same
time, and eat too if you didn't worry much about dribbling a bit
of strawberry and talking with your mouth open.

Greta was over at a friend's house and Mum was at the pet shop, picking up my mouse accessories for Greta and Tabitha's Christmas presents for Orlando and Brendan. Tabitha was helping Pamela with some sorting inside. They were apparently trying to find Christmas decorations but as none of the boxes were labelled this was very difficult.

"I saw your mother with Orlando and Brendan outside the other night," I said to Violet on the downward swing. "I saw them turn from kittens into boys," I added as we swung upwards.

"Yes, a fascinating process, isn't it?" Violet commented. "I was wondering if you realised that's where they are some of the time, running around doing kitteny things. Mother's getting a bit worried about them. They're supposed to be starting school next year but she doesn't want them to start until they have their kitten morphing under control. It's been a really strong urge for them, stronger than for the rest of us. And Orlando, well, even when he's in human form he meows.

"Mother's scared that Orlando will end up being a cat rather than a person, he changes so often. She's already lost my older brother that way."

She was silent as she took another bite of her strawberry.

"What happened to your older brother?" I asked after we

had gone downwards and upwards again on the swing, the bell on Violet's bracelet ringing softly with the motion.

After a very Violet pause she answered.

"Tom made the decision to be cat rather than human when he was sixteen and my parents were terribly upset. I mean, we still see him. I'm hoping he'll be home for Christmas, but Mother hasn't heard anything. We always have seafood at Christmas for him in case he comes. And he might stay a few days before he's off again. He doesn't mix in non-magical communities in any form except cat and Father in particular finds it insulting that he won't take human form even at Christmas lunch. He'll sit up on a chair at the table and just wave a paw if he wants another piece of fish. It's not so bad for the magical people in the family because we can understand what he is saying or thinking but Father has no idea. Tom doesn't come home as much as he used to though," Violet said. "He just doesn't understand why anyone would want to live in a non-magical community. He doesn't feel like he belongs here at all."

"So how many brothers or sisters do you have, Violet?" I asked. This was one of the problems in finding anything out from Violet. I would start with the aim of finding out a specific piece of information – in this case I wanted to know whether Violet herself could morph into a cat – but because there were so many interesting things about Violet and her family it was easy to become bogged down.

"I have four," she said. "One sister and three brothers: Tom, and then Tabitha who rarely changes, and the twins, who as you observed are in a state of transition at the moment."

"And what about you?" I asked. "Can you change into a cat?" Violet nodded.

"Do you do it often?"

Violet sighed. "I can change into a cat but I don't like to," she said. "And my parents don't really like me doing it either. When I change into a cat I'm a black cat." She said this like it explained something.

"What do you mean?" I asked. "What's worse about being a black cat than any other type of cat?"

"It's partly historical," she began, in her fake grown-up way. Luckily for her, what she was saying was so interesting that there was no space in my mind for irritation.

"Lots of people have gotten it wrong about lots of things to do with Creatures of Magic throughout the ages, but the whole black cat connection with magic is true. Black cats are more magical than any other type of cat."

"So . . .?" I asked. "Are you better at magic than most magical creatures?"

"Yes, I am a very skilled Creature of Magic," said Violet with no false modesty. "Even when I take cat form I can still perform quite strong magic, which is unusual. But because I'm a black cat I am also more noticeable."

"Really?" I said. "I wouldn't have thought a black cat was any more noticeable than other cats."

"They are," said Violet. "There are a lot of black cats around, but very few that are completely black. Most black cats will have small markings in another colour. Maybe just a bit of white around their whiskers, a white paw or a small spot of colour on their stomach. To be completely black with green eyes and black whiskers marks you as a magical creature and that can be dangerous. There are lots of people out there who want to get rid of us, and are actively searching for us. For me to turn into a cat is pretty much saying 'here I am, come and get me' and I don't want that to happen again."

"Again?" I asked. "Have these people caught you before?"

But Violet clammed up. It was a full-stop-rather-than-a-comma kind of silence.

"Do you want to help me unpack more books?" Violet asked.

"No, I might go home," I said, thinking Mum would probably be back with Greta's present.

"I was thinking you might like to borrow a book," Violet

said. "I had a particular book in mind. Given what you saw the other night, it might help you understand a few things."

"Is it a magical book?" I asked. "Would it be okay with your mother, do you think?"

"Oh, it would be no problem at all," said Pamela, appearing suddenly on the stairs. All of the Browns (except for John) had a very quick and quiet way of moving. At first I thought it was magical, the way they seemed to appear out of nowhere, but after watching them do it a number of times I realised they simply moved with stealth. The small bells on Pamela and Violet's bracelets were a clue to their presence, but the sound was soft and you had to be listening for it.

"Were you thinking of *Torture and Torment, Volume One*?" asked Pamela.

"Yes," said Violet. "Do you know where it is?"

Pamela closed her eyes for a minute and seemed to be thinking. A large book with golden writing appeared in her hands. Its full title was: *Torture and Torment — Everything You Need to Know About the Persecution of Creatures of Magic. Children's Edition, Volume One.* The cover featured a woman in black, weighed down with bricks, being thrown into a river.

"Feel free to come to me with any questions," Pamela said, handing me the book. "It might not be the best bedtime reading if you tend to have nightmares. Some parts are a bit scary."

There was nothing festive about *Torture and Torment, Volume One*. But it was interesting, very interesting, and as I always found it difficult to go to sleep on Christmas Eve, reading the book was a good time filler. Pamela's comment that the book was a bit scary was an understatement. It was petrifying. Despite its large text and simple language, it didn't seem to be a book appropriate for children. It wasn't something you would find in our school library, even in the section for older kids. There were graphic illustrations of the various methods that had been used to extract confessions of witchcraft from people, and some of them were very scary indeed. I skipped over most of the gory stuff.

I thought the history section might contain some interesting information, but even in large print it was difficult to plough through at night. Particularly on a hot night when I had a bedspread over the book to muffle the light of my torch. It took me until eleven o'clock to find anything that seemed relevant to the Browns' ability to morph into cats. There was a small section headed "Reaction to persecution – what Creatures of Magic did to protect themselves". It read:

The strong and loving relationship between Creatures of Magic and their cats has been comprehensively documented. (There were references here to a reading list that was long and boring.) *The method that one particular magical creature community adopted to escape torture and death has been less documented but was inspired by this strong relationship. Some secrecy has surrounded this method to ensure a degree of ongoing protection for the descendants of this community, who to this day retain an intimate relationship with our feline friends. To escape a particularly fierce "witch" hunt that took place in Cordeur, France in 1442, one community of magical creatures enclosed their community and cats in a particularly strong and comprehensive spell. This spell transformed all magical creatures in the community into a litter of kittens. To avoid detection this community remained in kitten and subsequently cat form for a number of years, some elderly members dying while still in cat form. As time passed some members forgot their original state and became unable to transform themselves back into human form. It is thought that there are still kittens today that are descendants of these cats, living in ignorance of their heritage and power.*

Luckily, the majority of the community remained focussed on their original identity as Creatures of Magic, even when forced into cat form for a number of years. Over the generations this community of cats/Creatures of Magic has retained the ability to transform into feline form quickly and easily, with some members making the lifestyle decision to choose cat form over human form.

Spontaneous conversion has proved to be a problem for some branches of the family, particularly when the magical creatures are at baby/kitten stage, when there appears to be little conscious control over spontaneous conversion into the feline state.

So the Browns must have descended from one of these

families, with Tom being an example of a Creature of Magic that had made the "lifestyle decision" to become a cat.

I wondered whether I would like to be cat. I could see some of the attractions — there was a lot of freedom, a lot of lazing in the sun and by the fire. There would be no homework or jobs, but also no chocolate or books or proper birthday parties. And I couldn't imagine wanting to eat mice. Yuck, just the thought was enough to make me feel physically sick. I decided that I was quite happy to be human.

14

Christmas, *noun* **festival of Christ's birth, 25 December, devoted esp. to family reunion and merrymaking, usually including presents.**

Santa Claus was efficient. Greta found a recycled iPad in her stocking and I had enough books to last me weeks, at least until the end of the summer holidays. Greta loved her new mouse toys and Sugar, Marmalade and Fuzzy did as well which was nice. They worked out how to use the toys Tabitha had chosen quickly and seemed to be enjoying themselves in a mouse-like way.

After a massive lunch with our grandparents, who lived a suburb or two away, Mum said we could go over to the Browns for a quick Christmas visit. Mum had settled on one lounge with a new book and Dad was peacefully snoring on the other, so Greta and I thought there would be some flexibility around the definition of "quick".

After knocking on the Browns' front door for ages, without

anyone answering, Greta and I decided to go over the back fence. We knew they were there because we could hear Brendan and Orlando shrieking with laughter and the rumble of grown-up voices. The back door was open so we went inside, followed the noise and learned how the Browns celebrated Christmas.

The front rooms had been completely transformed. There were rows and rows of red candles burning across the mantelpiece. Red wax was gaily dripping onto the floor and starting to melt the bubble-wrapped box that seemed to represent a cave.

Inside the cave was a nativity scene. I moved closer to look at it and realised that rather than the usual barn animals there were lots of plastic rats and mice in the straw. There were angels with wings and a few figures that looked like shepherds. I leaped back as a real mouse suddenly emerged from the straw, twitching its pink nose before darting across the room.

The downstairs taxidermic creatures had been given a festive look with tinsel and Christmas lights, and some of them even wore flashing Christmas tree earrings. There was a massive bowl of Pamela's strawberries on the table and chocolate wrappers were scattered across the floor. Sitting at the table, eating strawberries, was Uncle Roger. He was talking to Pamela and a pregnant woman with blond hair and bright green eyes.

"—bureau policy moving towards exile rather than return,

been a few tense meetings it seems. Been a bit of argy-bargy reading between the lines. Other Place pushing for the Bureau to deal with misdemeanours over here rather than transporting Creatures back when they muck up. Pammy, you're going to have to watch that mermaid while I'm away. Could be trouble, I reckon."

"Oh Rog, I think you're being a bit dramatic," said the green-eyed woman. "Charlene wouldn't really *hurt* anyone. Anyway, enough business talk. You're officially on holidays now!"

Roger winked at me and Greta. "Hello, girls. Think we might have met before. Roger's the name, protection of Creatures the game — and this is Olivia my wife."

"Oh Rog, you are SO corny!" said the woman. "Happy Christmas, girls!"

A paddling pool had been set up in the lounge room. Charlene was in there, wearing a bikini top covered with a print of Santa in swimmers, carrying a surfboard. She had a crown of flickering musical Christmas lights on her head, playing a tinny Christmas carol. I felt sure there were rules about electricity with water, something that meant danger, but this didn't seem to dampen the mood in the Browns' lounge room. Pamela and Charlene were playing a video game with Brendan. They were all having a great time, although when Charlene found herself losing she started splashing Brendan with water, irritating him no end.

Tabitha was singing karaoke by herself in the corner, following the words on a small screen and singing into a microphone. Charlene's eyes kept darting to the microphone and it looked like she was just biding her time before she wrested it away from Tabitha. Greta and I might need to make a quick exit if we didn't want to finish our Christmas in a coma.

The back wall was covered with coloured rock-climbing nooks, like the ones you have in an indoor rock-climbing centre, and Orlando was halfway up. Even in human form he climbed like a cat and was loving it, purring with each new foothold.

"Wow," Greta said, her eyes wide with excitement. She ran over to climb with Orlando.

John Brown was lying on the couch in a position similar to Dad, with his mouth open, snoring, despite the noise of Brendan laughing, the musical Christmas lights, Tabitha crooning like a cat in a fight, and Greta shouting at Orlando to move so she could reach certain footholds. Wocky was out of the cellar, the top part of his body lying beside John Brown on the couch. He had lifted his head and sniffed the air as Greta and I came into the room, but seemed content to lie back down and rest his drooling jaws close to John Brown's face.

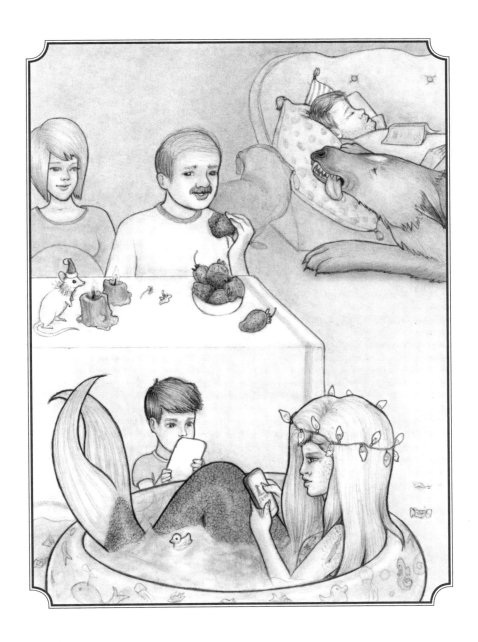

Roger moved to join in the video game, which involved pushing people dressed in black robes off a ship into the water – the more people you pushed off the more points you gained. "They're a bit Inquisitor-like, aren't they, Pammy?" he asked. "No wonder you're good at this."

The only person missing was Violet, and as she was the person I most wanted to see I went upstairs to find her. I had a small Christmas present for her.

Violet was in her very tidy bedroom, looking out the window at the sky. I climbed up onto her bed to join her, putting the present down at the end of the bed. I didn't want to make a big thing of it, because I didn't want her to feel bad if she hadn't bought or made a present for me. It was only a small thing, one of those balls that you shake and snow falls down. This one was special because it was floating sand falling down on a pretty black cat on the beach.

"Happy Christmas," I said. "What are you thinking?"

"Oh, nothing much," she said. She sounded a bit sad which didn't seem right at Christmas time.

"What did you get for Christmas?" I asked.

"Some good plastic stuff," Violet said. "No loom, but I did get little Oscar who's more fun anyway." I looked down at her lap and saw a tiny kitten with a creamy white coat and a small patch of tabby on his back. She was rubbing his shoulders and he was purring.

"Are you sure that's not one of the twins?" I joked.

Violet scrutinised Oscar. "No, I'm sure he's not one of the twins," she said seriously, "and I don't think he's a transmogrified Creature of Magic."

I wondered how many of the cats I knew were potentially Creatures of Magic. It was a wonderful thought. I scratched Oscar between the ears.

Violet started talking. "I'm disappointed Tom didn't make it here for Christmas. Thinking about it makes me feel sad, and living here sometimes makes me feel sad. It's just not really what I thought it would be like, living in a mixed magical and non-magical community with my family. I mean it's probably better, heaps better than last time anyway, but ..." Her voice trailed off.

I left a nice little well of silence. Violet had shown me that if you left the space for someone to speak, they would generally fill it with words, and Violet eventually did.

"I mean it's heaps more fun than I thought it would be, and it's great having you as a friend, and Father and Tabitha seem really happy ... But I still want to go back to the Other Place. I keep worrying that we're not safe here. I'm always looking over my shoulder, and the fact that no one else seems to be worried just makes me worry more."

"Well, I just met Roger downstairs. I don't think he'd let anything happen to you, and I don't think Charlene would let too much get past her either," I said, trying to cheer Violet up. "She'd be a pretty good watchdog."

"Watch creature," corrected Violet. "And that's the idea really. That's one of the reasons I summoned her."

The sound of Mum calling over the back fence meant that it was time to go home. Although the scene of Christmas fun downstairs was wonderful, I wasn't sure whether Mum would appreciate this wonder. I didn't want her coming into the Browns' house to look for us, so dragging a reluctant Greta with me I went home.

It had been a good Christmas and the nicest part of it was at the end of the day when I snuggled into bed with one of my new books. A soft summer rain was falling and there were a few low-lying clouds in the sky that turned pink with the sunset. As I watched their shape changed. I rubbed my eyes. I thought I must be mistaken — there must be an aeroplane writing a message. First there was a "w" followed by an "i" and an "s". It was only at the last word that I realised what was happening. It was Violet's Christmas present to me — a

Christmas card written in cloudwriting. It said "Wishing you a crevasse Christmas Anna", followed by a small picture of a cat. I wondered who else had seen my message and if any other Anna thought it was for her.

15

Compromise, *noun* a solution to a problem
where no one is thrilled, but everyone is resigned;
a fair way of working things out.

The day after Christmas I woke up to the sound of Pamela and John Brown arguing in the backyard. They were sitting at their barbecue table having breakfast.

"She has to go," John Brown said firmly. "She simply cannot play my harp and I can't stand having her permanently in the bathroom. She watches me while I shave and hums under her breath. Sometimes my hand shakes so much I cut myself. And Wocky has not been the same since she's been around. Every time she makes a sound the fur on his back rises. He's having trouble sleeping and his tummy has been upset. I don't know if the crepe myrtle will survive."

"Oh John," Pamela said, her bracelet tinkling as she stirred her cup of catmint tea. "Don't be such a wimp. And what do you mean 'just get rid of her'? You know I can't use magic. We need to learn how to manage life with Charlene."

"I cannot 'manage'!" John Brown said, his voice rising with anger. "Isn't there a zoo for accidentally created magical creatures that she can be sent to? Hire a boat and dump her in the ocean somewhere if you have to. Donate her as a raffle prize for the Retired Naval Officers League! Get rid of her!"

He was starting to lose it.

"And what sort of message do you think that would give the children?" Pamela asked, taking a sip of her tea. "They have summoned her; they need to look after her. And what do you think the Bureau would say? We're lucky we've got Roger there and that he's prepared to dismiss Violet's summoning of Charlene as childish mischief rather than a magical misdemeanour. But if I used magic to get rid of her, we could be in big trouble. It's like Wocky really — just as he is our responsibility, she is our responsibility."

"You can't use Wocky as a case in point, Pamela," John Brown mocked. "You wanted to leave the poor animal behind."

"But we didn't, John, did we?" said Pamela. "And I'm glad you insisted — it was the right thing to bring Wocky with us. Although I think you could walk him more often, as you agreed to when we decided to bring him."

John Brown rolled his eyes. "I walk that animal every second night no matter how late it is when I get home. And quite frankly I don't understand why it's left to me, the only non-nocturnal member of the household, to walk Wocky in the middle of the night when all I want to do is go to sleep!"

"We agreed, John," Pamela said, "that we would try as much as possible to get the children into a routine more suitable to the environment in which we are currently living, which means we have to put them to bed at night. We all find that difficult, darling, just as you found it difficult being up all night at the Other Place. But getting back to Charlene, I think it's very good for the children to have someone they are responsible for, you know, having someone else to look after."

"Pamela, she is DANGEROUS!" John Brown shouted.

"Arthur and Rita Raton are dangerous – Charlene just needs to be managed in a more appropriate manner," Pamela explained. "I agree, the upstairs bathroom is no place for a mermaid. Anyone would go crazy living in that tiny room. She needs a bigger area to swim in, some company, and social training about how to interact with people in a way that doesn't involve luring them to their death. She needs to train that voice of hers and maybe I should buy her some more bikini tops. I'm glad you've brought it up really, because I've thought of a solution that could help Charlene, and at the same time help the children with some of their issues."

"Anything to get that mermaid away from the bathroom and my harp," groaned John Brown.

"What about a swimming pool in the backyard?" said Pamela. "We have room."

"So you're suggesting we keep her in our backyard in a swimming pool?" asked John. "We would have to have a very big fence around it so people couldn't see her."

I could tell he was considering it.

"It would be wonderful for the children, John, wonderful. Imagine, we might even be able to teach them to swim!" Pamela enthused.

"I doubt they'll put a toe into the water voluntarily," John said. He sighed. "Whatever — anything to get her out of the bathroom."

I smiled. Violet and Tabitha having a pool in their backyard would almost be as good as us having one in our backyard. I loved swimming. I leaped out of bed and got dressed. I couldn't wait to tell Violet the news — I realised she would hardly be as excited as me, given her dislike of water, but I was sure Charlene moving from the bathroom would make her happy.

16

Obstreperous, *adjective* good description for behaviour typically engaged in by small boys that they think is funny, but is really naughty and infuriating.

It was the first week of January and Mum had asked Pamela and the kids over for afternoon tea. Brendan, Orlando and Greta were playing upstairs with Sugar, Marmalade and Fuzzy, and Tabitha had ducked outside to find some twigs and grass, "to help the mice hide" she explained. Violet stayed with me and the grown-ups. Mum was asking Pamela how she had met John, Violet's father, and Pamela was enjoying telling the story. "We met at a party," she said. "He was playing in a band there, but I met him while he was on a break. I thought he said he was a magician but he was really saying he was a musician. A lucky mistake. It was his name that really drew me in though."

"His name?" asked Mum. "His name is John, isn't it, John Brown?"

"Yes," Pamela said dreamily. "John Brown. It's such a plain

name, and once we started talking I realised there was nothing magic about him — it felt *dangerous* and I knew right then he was the person for me."

"All that is gold does not glitter," said Violet.

Mum raised an eyebrow.

"He was extraordinarily ordinary!" Pamela enthused. "And now here we are, living such an ordinary life!"

Mum and Pamela both took a sip of their tea.

"I love your brooch," Mum said. "Violet has one that's similar, I noticed it when we were on the train the other day. Can I have a look at yours?"

Pamela moved closer to Mum so she could see the brooch clearly. "Thanks, Dorothy," she said. "I rarely take it off as it has great sentimental value — my parents gave it to me. The children love it too."

"So how many children do you have, Pamela?" asked Mum.

"Oh, about five at any given time," said Pamela. "It's a fluid population."

"In what way exactly?" queried Mum.

"Well, you know, children come and go!" Pamela said. I could see she was struggling. I knew what she meant by fluid population.

"One of Pamela's children has left home already," I explained to Mum in a flash of inspiration. I looked to Violet for help but she said nothing.

"Yes, Tom is currently travelling," Pamela added, eyeing the flower arrangement at the centre of the table.

"He's always travelling. He doesn't like us much," Tabitha commented on her way upstairs to join Greta, carrying an armful of twigs and grass.

"Dear me. Are you sure you need all those sticks?" Mum asked.

"Oh yes," said Tabitha, earnestly. "Brendan and Orlando get very *excited* playing with the mice. They wouldn't mean to hurt them, but if the mice have a few more places to hide ..."

"All right," Mum said. "Just make sure the sticks and grass stay in the mouse cage and not on the floor."

"Of course, Dorothy," Tabitha promised as she made her way up the stairs, leaving a trail of grass cuttings behind her.

Mum sighed, resigned to the mess. She resumed her conversation with Pamela.

"But what do you mean about your son Tom?" Mum asked. "Don't you see him?"

"I'd rather not talk about such unpleasantness. No point dwelling on the sadnesses of family life, or the past, however unfortunate it might be," Pamela answered briskly. "What beautiful flowers, Dorothy," she said, changing the subject. "They look good enough to eat."

I gently moved the vase away from Pamela.

"I wouldn't mind a cutting of your sage," Pamela added, trying again. "I haven't had a lot of success with mine and yours looks quite robust."

"Yes," Mum said. "It's going really well this year. I tell you what though, that crepe myrtle out the front has just gone ballistic this summer. I think it's grown about a third of a metre. And the flowers on it, I've never seen anything like them!"

As the adult conversation drifted into safer (and more boring) channels about plants, gardening, water restrictions and the benefits of mulching, I relaxed. Maybe Mum and Mrs Brown could become friends. I daydreamed about shared family camping holidays, picnics and trips to the beach.

These pleasant reveries were unfortunately cut short by the entrance of Greta, screaming, "They're eating my mice! Please, Mummy, come and save my mice!"

Brendan trailed after Greta. He had Fuzzy hanging out of his mouth and he was holding Sugar in his hands. Tightly. Greta's mice looked like they were about to die of heart failure if they weren't ingested first.

Looking at Brendan I thought for one terrible moment that

he was morphing from a boy into a kitten in front of Mum. I knew Pamela was anxious, thinking the same thing, but I think we quickly came to the same conclusion. He had been a kitten and must have changed back into a boy mid-mouse chase. He dropped Sugar onto the floor and I wondered whether his puzzled expression meant he was unsure what was in his mouth. Fuzzy's tail was poking out, flicking from side to side. Using his thumb and forefinger, Brendan delicately removed the mouse from his mouth and dropped it on the floor next to Sugar. Fuzzy looked very flat. But he was alive. He sat stunned on the kitchen floor. Tabitha hurried down the stairs and picked up Sugar and gave her to Greta, who cradled her in her hands.

"You awful, awful boy," Greta screamed. "What do you think you're doing eating my mice? Go eat your own mice at your own house!"

I glanced at Violet who was unperturbed by the drama unfolding around her.

"Do your children have mice as well, Pamela?" Mum asked, her eyebrows locked a centimetre above their usual resting position.

"Oh yes," said Tabitha. "We have lots and lots of mice, some that are pets and some that are, well, not so much pets as—"

"Yes, we do keep mice," Pamela said. "We have more mice

than children at the moment," she said as she swooped to the floor with one of her silent, sudden movements and collected poor Fuzzy, who appeared frozen with fear. She handed the wet mouse to Tabitha.

"Now, Brendan, could you please apologise to Greta for playing with her mice in such a silly way," she ordered.

"Yes, Brendan," added Tabitha, feeling the need to put her bit in defending her friend's mice. "They are pets, Brendan. They are different to the mice that we keep in the walls at our place."

"Sorry, Greta," Brendan mumbled.

Tabitha and Greta stormed upstairs and as Brendan turned to follow, I realised with horror that he still had his kitten's tail poking out from the top of his jeans. I glanced across at Mum who, thankfully, was passing Pamela some more biscuits and seemed a bit distracted, probably by Tabitha's remarks about the mice in the walls next door. As I watched, his tail retreated into itself and disappeared, and at the top of the stairs he hitched his jeans up over the spot where the tail had been just moments before.

"Now, Pamela, if you have a pest problem, we would be very happy to share the cost of eradication," Mum said.

Pamela looked puzzled.

I looked to Violet to help me out. She didn't.

"Mum's talking about the mice in the walls," I explained. This was a mistake.

"How kind of you, Dorothy. But the mice don't bother me at all. If we feel the numbers are getting excessive, we just, we just—" Pamela looked at Mum's horrified face and my very worried one and rethought what she wanted to say.

Violet giggled.

"What I mean is we don't have an issue with pest control, we just prefer to use more natural methods. I don't like pesticides in the garden and I certainly wouldn't use any kind of poison in my house," Pamela concluded.

Mum's face brightened. "I couldn't agree more, Pamela. Only the other day I read something about mice extermination and a clever trap method involving two boxes, a skewer, a roll of toilet paper and some peanut butter. Anyway, I'm so happy we can have a conversation about these things. Our old neighbour, Rita Raton, was difficult to talk to about anything. It's problematic when you share a boundary fence and have a common wall."

Pamela murmured sympathetically and said she had some mail for Rita Raton. She asked Mum if she had an address Pamela could forward the letters to.

"I'll give it to them if you like," Mum said. "Funnily enough, they are dropping by here tomorrow. Rita Raton called me yesterday and said that they were in town and wanted to know whether they could drop something off to us. I don't know what it is. I was surprised when she called — they were such quiet people. We didn't have a lot to do with them."

Pamela's hand shook and she spilled her tea.

"Oh, silly me," she said brightly. Her hand was still shaking as she helped Mum mop up the tea.

I turned to Violet, who had been quiet through both the Brendan-mouse interruption and Mum and Pamela's conversation. She now looked very tense. Her hands were holding her cup of tea very tightly and if she had been in cat form, I'm sure she would have been swishing her tail.

"Do you want to come outside with me, Violet?" I asked, curious about what had upset my friend. "Mum, can we put on our togs and turn the hose on?"

"You can hold the hose, Violet," I added, looking at her screwed up face. "Look, we don't need to play with the hose at all. I need to talk to you," I whispered to her. "Come on!"

"Yes, yes, whatever," said Mum, still talking to Pamela about Rita Raton.

Violet was listening very intently. What could she possibly find so interesting about our old neighbours?

"Come on, Violet," I said, standing up behind her. Violet

ignored me. It was only when Mum had finished describing Rita Raton's shortcomings — "she never came to the street Christmas party" — that she stood up and followed me outside. We sat on the trampoline.

"What's wrong, Vi?" I asked. "Why are you so interested in Rita Raton?"

Violet looked at me and I was shocked to see that her eyes were full of tears.

"You don't understand, Anna," she said. "She's a bad person, Rita Raton, and Arthur, well, he is evil. I thought they were gone and I could protect my family, but I don't know whether that's possible. I don't have much time before tomorrow. I'm going to have to go home and work something out."

"What do you mean, work something out?" I asked. "What has Rita Raton to do with you? She's just coming here to drop something off to Mum, probably something really boring. And who is Arthur?"

Violet was silent.

"And anyway," I added. "How do you even know Rita Raton? She'd been gone for ages before you moved in."

"Trust me," said Violet. "Our family knows Rita Raton better than any of us would like. I know who she is and what she does to magical creatures."

"I know her," I said. "She's not the friendliest of people but that doesn't make her evil."

"Appearances can be deceiving," Violet said. "I don't have time to explain now — I knew we couldn't trust the Bureau to protect us. I have to go. If Rita Raton asks about us tomorrow, can you tell her we've gone on holiday, suddenly and unexpectedly? Tell her someone in the family has died, that might be better, and we've all had to go to the country for a funeral. Tell your Mum beforehand so it sounds real. I need to depart."

And depart she did. She was over the back fence in seconds and I heard the faint sound of the Browns' back door opening.

I wandered back inside, wondering whether Violet had gone crazy.

Greta flounced back downstairs. She had wrapped Fuzzy the mouse in toilet paper. He looked a bit like he had been mummified, with his little face poking out from his bandaged torso, arms and legs. He was still alive, thank goodness. If he had died of shock, I don't think Greta would have spoken to anyone in the Brown house again, rock-climbing wall or no rock-climbing wall.

"He's still alive," she announced to Mum and Pamela. "No thanks to Brendan though. I don't think he should come over here any more."

"Not until he's got his appetite for mice under control anyway," agreed Pamela. "Where is he?"

"He's playing with my Lego," said Greta. "But I think he should probably go home now."

"Greta, that's not very polite," Mum admonished.

"No, she's right, we really should get going," said Pamela. "There are some more books I want to unpack today and I think Violet has already gone home. Thanks for the tea, Dorothy. Brendan! Orlando! Tabitha! Come downstairs please, we're going."

"Do you still have that book I gave you, Anna?" Pamela said to me quietly as she was walking out the front door. "Read chapter eleven, it might explain why Violet is so upset."

17

Scapegoat, *noun* someone who is blamed for everything that goes wrong even if they had nothing to do with it.

I had to wait until night-time before I could have a good read of the book. Greta and I were doing a week of swimming classes, and because of the heat we stayed on at the swimming pool. I didn't want anyone else to see the book, so it wasn't until Greta was asleep that I finally got it out. I hadn't heard or seen anything of Violet or Tabitha for the rest of the day. I presumed that Violet was busy Raton-proofing her house.

The whole street seemed to have gone away. The only people around wore long black-hooded robes, and walked past our house a few times each day. I had seen the same people — three of them — down at the shops earlier in the week. They looked out of place with their heavy hooded robes in the summer heat. Mum thought a monastery had relocated to our suburb somewhere. I wasn't so sure. The way the robes hid the people's faces was creepy. And they reminded me of something.

I couldn't quite put my finger on what, but it wasn't monks.

Chapter eleven was hard work and I didn't understand why Pamela referred me to it. I struggled to read, post-swimming tiredness threatening to close my eyes.

Although the assault on Creatures of Magic (formerly known as witches) was most intense during the 1400s, their persecution has continued well into the present day. Despite growing tolerance in subsequent centuries, Creatures of Magic have never enjoyed the complete acceptance of the wider non-magical community.

A small unit of non-magical creatures known as the Inquisitors has continued to secretly hunt and persecute Creatures of Magic in the name of "community good". The impact of the Inquisitors' hate crimes has thankfully been reduced by this group's traditional deficits in planning, coordination and insight. Their desire for anonymity is often thwarted by their traditional dress of black robes with hoods, which although commonplace in the Other Place, has made subterfuge problematic in the non-magical world. The obvious enjoyment gained by the Inquisitors by wearing this traditional garb and the aura of mystery this creates has worked to alert Creatures of Magic to the whereabouts of their traditional enemy in the context of the non-magical world.

Provocation to perform magic is one strategy used by this group to enforce Creature of Magic exclusion from the non-magical community. Inquisitors will also steal magical emblems or other evidence of magical reality to prompt Creature of Magic exile from the non-magical community. Shamefully,

Inquisitors have also stolen infant Creatures of Magic in an attempt to break the cycle of transmission of magical knowledge. This practice seems to be increasing in recent times, with Inquisitors crossing the border from their world to the Other Place and taking babies back to the non-magical world. After an epidemic of such crimes the Bureau for the Protection of Creatures of Magic was established to serve the twin functions of protection of Creatures of Magic and their families and monitoring of adherence to the Charter of Magical Doings, 1300.

Scapegoating of Creatures of Magic is an ancient tradition continued by the Inquisitors into the modern day. Inquisitors believe that individual magical creatures have harmed individual members of the larger community through their performance of "spells". This is of course nonsense. Creatures of Magic strictly adhere to the Charter of Magical Doings, 1300, *which explicitly forbids the use of magic without a permit in the mixed (magical and non-magical) communities. Granting of such permits has been governed by increasingly strict criteria. Failure to adhere to the Charter can result in enforced return to the Other Place or other forms of exile from non-magical communities.*

Despite concerted efforts by the magical community, negotiation with the Inquisitors has traditionally been problematic and effective mediation between the Inquisitors and Creatures of Magic has now broken down completely. Many Creatures of Magic, particularly those living in mixed (magical and non-magical) communities have lived in fear of persecution by the Inquisitors. As a result of concerted lobbying by Creatures of Magic, the non-magical world has introduced its own penalties for Inquisitorial victimisation of Creatures of Magic occurring in the non-magical world. The Bureau for the Protection of Creatures of Magic has in recent times received increased government funding to reflect its expanding functions. Due to the sensitive nature of magic in the context of the non-magical community, the nature of this taskforce has been kept secret from all but the highest levels of government.

Yes, the Bureau. From what I had seen I could understand why Violet didn't have too much confidence in them, not if they were all like Roger with his weak jokes and inability to ward off mermaids. If this was the case, I understood why Violet felt so strongly that she needed to protect her family from the Inquisitors.

Inquisitors have been known to capture Creatures of Magic and prosecute them in their own Inquisitorial court. Forcible confiscation of magical emblems by the Inquisitors is common practice in these courts and other, darker methods are rumoured to have been used to limit the population of Creatures of Magic. While many in the magical community argue that magic should be able to be used more freely as a weapon against the Inquisitors, strict laws continue to govern the circumstances under which magic can be used against non-magical creatures. Recent amendments to magical law have allowed for magic to be used only when a Creature of Magic is placed in extreme peril because of the actions of a non-magical creature. The definition of extreme peril continues to be debated in the courts.

Peril was a strong word. How bad did something have to be before it was considered perilous? I sleepily wondered why Violet was so worried about Rita Raton. Could she be an Inquisitor? And what about magical emblems, what exactly were they? I fought my tiredness and looked in the index at the back of the book for the word "emblem". There were a lot of references. I turned to page 33 and read:

The significance of the tenth birthday for a young Creature of Magic is typically recognised by the awarding of a brooch known as an "emblem". This emblem is symbolic of the growing maturity of the young Creature of Magic and holds its own unique magical properties.

I thought of Pamela's and Violet's cat brooches. They must be emblems.

For Creatures of Magic with strong cat transformation tendencies this emblem is particularly useful as a compass for orientating Creatures of Magic to their true and original state. When a Creature of Magic changes state to cat form there is always the risk that if they remain in this form for long they will forget they are Creatures of Magic. When a Creature of Magic possesses a magical emblem this emblem will remain in a consistent form, immune to the magic of transmogrification. The emblem, while being an anchor for the transmogrified Creature of Magic, also acts to alert the trained observer to the true identity of an emblem wearing feline.

Some sectors of Creature of Magic society see emblems as a symbol of social control, instigated by non-magical creatures to track the movements of Creatures of Magic in the non-magical community. The Bureau for the Protection of Creatures of Magic requires Creatures of Magic over the age of ten to wear their emblems at all times whether in human or feline form.

That was the last thing I remembered reading that night.

18

Retreat, *verb* to go away from a place or person
in order to escape from fighting or danger.

I slept in the next morning. Everyone had already had breakfast by the time I got out of bed and Mum was bustling around cleaning up.

"Good morning, sleepyhead," she said. "You'll be pleased to know I've just found one of your overdue library books under the couch."

"When are the Ratons coming, Mum?" I asked as I poured some cereal into a bowl.

"They'll probably be over soon. Rita Raton said sometime between ten and eleven," Mum said. "Oh, I meant to tell you that Violet popped by this morning. She dropped off some mail for Rita Raton and said the whole family were going to the country for a funeral. There's been a death in Pamela's family. They left early this morning. Pamela looked amazing, she had the most beautiful piece of black lace over her head.

"The little boys looked very cute in their black dinner suits, although those bow ties with mice all over them were a bit tacky," Mum continued. "Odd clothes for the funeral, but then that's the Browns. I suppose they are a bit . . ." Mum stopped.

I knew she was about to say "odd" but had thought better of it.

Mum sighed. "They are an unusual family," she said. "But fun, good fun."

"Yes," I said, thankful that Mum had no idea how unusual they really were.

There was a knock at the door and Mum went to answer it.

"Oh, Rita," I heard her say. "You're early. Come in, how nice to see you."

I looked at the clock. It was only 9.30. Rita Raton was early. She was that kind of person. An early person. I imagined her house as being orderly, full of folded laundry put neatly away in cupboards, and meals served with military precision to clean children who always remembered to say "please" and "thank you" and never spilled food on their clothing.

I wondered what Rita Raton would think if she could see inside her old house now. Violet made an effort to put things away but she was the only person in the family who seemed to have any respect for order and tidiness, so her efforts didn't make much of a dent in the chaos that characterised their house.

Rita Raton sat down at the table with her two children. Edward and Emily gazed with big eyes at the chocolate biscuits Mum had brought out but neither attempted to touch them.

"Would you like a cup of tea or coffee, Rita?" Mum asked, breaking the silence.

"Why thank you, Dorothy," Rita Raton said, reaching into her bag and bringing out a small lunch box full of thinly sliced apple and wholemeal sandwiches, which she gave to Edward and Emily. I watched as they dutifully chewed on their apple, resigned to their morning tea.

I reached for a biscuit and could feel Rita Raton's disapproval. I realised I still had my pyjamas on.

"Chocolate biscuits for breakfast, Anna?" she asked in her quiet voice.

"Only during the school holidays," said Mum, returning with a pot of tea and a small jug of milk.

Mum poured the tea. "So how are you finding your new house, Rita?" she queried.

"Yes, we are really enjoying it, thank you, Dorothy. We're flanked by national park on two sides, so it is very private and we're not troubled by any nosy neighbours," said Rita Raton, declining the offered chocolate biscuits.

Mum put her teacup down loudly. Her face had a tight look.

"Our new neighbours are just lovely — they are so sociable. In fact if they weren't out at a funeral today they would probably be here now — chatting, you know, exchanging questions and answers in a friendly way, as some neighbours do."

Rita frowned. She did not speak. As I may have said before, she was a better note writer than talker — as our next door neighbour she had always preferred notes to actual conversation. I wondered whether, if I slipped a note to Rita Raton to read while she drank her cup of tea, she would write something back and slip it to me and we could have a conversation that way. Looking at Rita's stern face I decided it was unlikely.

Ginger had slunk into the room while we were talking and now he tried to jump onto Emily's lap. Really he was the most contrary cat. He showed me absolutely no affection, even though I was the person feeding him every night, and here he was snuggling up to a small child who he didn't know.

Rita Raton jumped up from her seat and grabbed Ginger out of Emily's lap. Before Mum or I could say or do anything she tossed him out the back door. We looked out the door, shocked. Mum's jaw dropped.

"Emily and Edward have cat allergies," Rita Raton said, wiping her hands with disinfectant she had taken from her bag.

"I can't have them near cats at any time."

Ginger's ejection had not been gentle. Mum frowned and took a deep breath. "It's a myth that cats always fall on their feet," she said.

Rita Raton raised her eyebrows and changed the subject.

"Dorothy, I have the invoice here for the fencing work I had done prior to our move. I thought you might like to contribute given it is a boundary fence." Rita Raton started to look through her handbag for the invoice.

Mum rolled her eyes — well, at least we knew now why Rita Raton wanted to speak to us.

"I'm disappointed to hear the new people are out," said Rita Raton, handing over the invoice. "I left something behind when we moved and I had been hoping to go inside to have a look. I don't suppose you have a contact number for them Dorothy, or even a spare key?"

Mum frowned.

"I don't think so, Rita," she said. "Pamela has gone to a funeral today so I really don't think it's right to call her, and in any case I wouldn't feel comfortable going into their house without her."

"So you have a spare key for next door?" Rita Raton said, looking excited.

"Yes," said Mum a little tersely. "You are surely not suggesting, Rita, that I let you into their house while they're away?"

I got the feeling that Mum did not trust Rita Raton. She would never let her into the Browns' house without their permission.

"Yes," said Rita Raton. "I mean no. Do you mind if I use your bathroom?"

"Not at all," said Mum. "You know where it is."

As Rita Raton made her way towards the bathroom, Edward and Emily continued to sit in silence and chew their apple.

"Do you want a chocolate biscuit?" Mum asked Emily.

"I'm not allowed to eat chocolate," Emily whispered.

They looked sweet and forlorn, the Raton children sitting at the table. They weren't upset like some small children would be if their mother left them in a strange room. Was it my imagination, or did they seem more relaxed?

"Did you have a nice Christmas, Emily?" I asked.

"Not really," whispered Emily.

"Why's that?" Mum asked, moving closer to the little girl. "Did Santa leave you some lovely presents?"

"No," said Edward. It was the first word he had said since entering our house. He spoke as softly as his sister.

"Santa Claus left us a letter," said Emily.

"We bad," said Edward sadly. "No Santa pwesents."

"Next year we will be better," said Emily. She squared her small shoulders.

"What did you do?" I asked, finding it difficult to imagine these two quiet, model children doing anything even remotely naughty, let alone something on the scale of naughtiness that could warrant no Christmas presents.

"Santa said in his letter that we were being too noisy and did not do what Mummy asked us to do," said Emily.

"Vewy messy bedwoom," said Edward.

"And we fought over Edward's crayon," said Emily, holding her little brother's hand.

Edward looked close to tears.

Mum gathered him up in her arms.

"Now you listen to me children," she said. "I'm sure there must have been some kind of mistake with Santa's letter. I'm sure ..." Mum looked at me. I could see she was struggling. "Here, have a chocolate biscuit," she said, passing a biscuit to Edward. "I'll tell Mummy I said it was all right. And you too, Emily."

It wasn't until Edward and Emily had finished their biscuits that I realised Rita Raton had been gone a long time, a lot longer than any visit to a toilet that wasn't your own should take.

Mum was thinking the same thing.

"Go and check on her, Anna," she said. "Make sure she's okay."

I thought Rita Raton was more likely to be up to mischief than suffering some kind of tummy upset.

The downstairs toilet door was wide open. Maybe she'd decided the downstairs bathroom did not reach her high standards of cleanliness and had chosen to use the toilet upstairs?

As I bounded up the stairs I heard a sound that I knew well. It was the unmistakable creaking of the attic ladder being cranked back into place. My steps became quieter and more Violet-like as I checked the upstairs bathroom. Rita Raton wasn't there. I could hear footsteps. She could only be in Mum and Dad's bedroom or the bedroom I shared with Greta. I quietly stepped behind the bathroom door and closed it until there was only a small crack to peer through. And what I saw was very interesting. Rita Raton emerged from my bedroom. She was smoothing her skirt down with one hand and I heard her curse when she noticed she had a ladder in her skin-toned stockings.

As she walked past my hiding place I caught a glimpse of a book with gold writing on it, poking out of her bag.

I gasped. Could Rita Raton have found *Torture and Torment — Everything You Need to Know About the Persecution of Creatures of Magic, Children's Edition, Volume One*?

I thought I had hidden it carefully enough to escape both Greta's and Mum's curious eyes. I had wrapped it in an old T-shirt and placed it inside the bottom cupboard in my bedroom. The door to this cupboard tended to get stuck and it was filled with clothes that were rarely worn, like winter clothes that weren't needed in summer. I waited until Rita Raton had reached the bottom of the stairs and then ran to my bedroom and checked for the book. It was still there.

As I carefully closed the cupboard door I thought about the book in Rita Raton's bag. It had looked familiar. The gold, honeyish writing was something I had seen before. But where? It came to me. It was the book of spells that Violet had used to summon Charlene. Rita Raton must have used the ladder in our bedroom to climb into the Browns' house. She had stolen the book of spells.

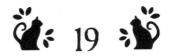

19

Protect, *verb* to keep something safe, and when you can't do this sometimes taking action to defend it.

While Rita Raton wiped Emily's and Edward's faces, I tiptoed behind her. I slipped my hand into her bag and probed for the book of spells. With trembling fingers I started to ease it out — then she turned and saw me. Angrily, she pulled the bag close to her. I tried to push my hand back inside but Rita slapped it away.

"Rita! Anna! What do you think you're doing?" Mum asked, dragging me away. Reckless, I lunged at Rita Raton, but Mum held onto me. Edward hid his face in Emily's dress.

"Goodbye, Dorothy," Rita Raton said in an injured voice. "Give my regards to your husband Michael, and I suggest you teach your daughter some manners." She grabbed Emily's and Edward's hands and left.

"What is going on, Anna?" Mum asked, mystified.

I mumbled something about a missing book, but when Mum

pressed me I didn't say anything else. She sent me up to my bedroom.

I knew Violet was going to be terribly upset.

Being alone in my room gave me time to think. Violet and I were going to have to get that book back. My mood brightened as I thought about this. I remembered how the book *Torture and Torment — Everything You Need to Know About the Persecution of Creatures of Magic, Children's Edition, Volume One*, had magically appeared in Pamela's hands when she wanted it. Surely the same method could be used to retrieve the book of spells?

❋

The Browns arrived back in their Tarago three days later, still wearing black. Pamela emerged looking hot, dusty and tired, with the black lace scarf over her head.

Violet, Tabitha, Brendan and Orlando trailed out of the car after their mother.

Violet waved wearily to me as she walked into their house.

"Vi, I've got to talk to you," I said, following her inside.

"Not now, Anna," said Pamela, turning around. "We are all very tired, and the children need to have a shower or at least some contact with a face washer and go to bed."

Baths and bedtime weren't a strongly featured ritual in the Brown house, but looking at Pamela's face I knew she meant what she said.

"Goodnight, Anna," she said, showing me outside. "I'm sure Violet will be over to see you in the morning."

It was frustrating. I so wanted to tell Violet about the book. I knew it was important. We had swimming lessons again in the morning and I didn't want to wait until after lunch to speak to my friend.

Thinking how to do this kept me awake that night. Mum and Dad had gone to bed and I could hear Dad snoring. Greta was sleeping peacefully as well. It is a lonely feeling being the only person in your family awake. But the more I tried to relax my body into sleep the more alert I became. I couldn't relax until I had told Violet about Rita Raton. I toyed with the idea of going through the attic into Violet's bedroom but I was worried that the creaking sound would wake Mum and Dad.

I looked out my window into the Browns' backyard. It was almost a full moon so there was good visibility. I noticed something that made me sit still. Violet was creeping into the backyard. She was holding a long rope and seemed to be pulling something down their back steps. It must have been heavy because the thick rope was pulled taut. I guessed it was Wocky.

I leaned out the window. "Violet," I called in a loud whisper.

Violet's hearing was as good as her mother's. It was probably a cat thing. She looked up at me quickly, put her finger to her lips and gestured for me to climb over into their yard. I watched as she knotted the rope very firmly to one of the jacaranda trees. The rope was now less taut. I could hear Wocky snuffling and snorting under the trees. I slowly made my way downstairs, trying to make my steps as quiet and Violet-like as possible and taking special care to shut the back door quietly. I jumped over the fence.

"Father asked me to give Wocky a run around the backyard," Violet said.

I went forwards to pat Wocky, but Violet pulled on the rope to move him away from me.

"Take care!" she said. "He's more active at night and he's hungry."

I laughed nervously.

"Well, I'm sure he won't eat me!"

Violet's silence was her reply.

I quickly drew back.

"Anna, if he was in the wild, he'd be hunting at night. I mean, he comes from a family of hunters, poor hunters admittedly hence their near extinction, but he could still hurt you while attempting to catch you."

I let Violet come to me.

"How did the visit go, by the way? How was the awful Rita Raton?"

"Oh, Violet," I said.

Violet frowned.

"What is it, Anna?" she asked. "Did she do something bad to you? What happened?"

"Oh, Violet," I said again. I knew she was going to be really upset. "I'm afraid Rita Raton did manage to get into your house."

"Good heavens!" exclaimed Violet. "You can't tell me she managed to get past Wocky and Charlene and leave unharmed!"

"Well, she put a ladder in her stockings which I think distressed her," I said. "But yes, she did. She went in through the attic. Charlene mustn't have heard her because it's on the next level and Wocky wouldn't have heard her either because she came through the ceiling rather than the front door. She wasn't in there for very long."

Violet's face was very white.

"What did she take?" she whispered. Her hands were clenched together tightly and the bell on her bracelet was for once still.

"A book," I said miserably.

"Not *Torture and Torment — Everything You Need to Know About the Persecution of Creatures of Magic, Children's Edition, Volume One?*" Violet whispered.

"No, that's what I thought at first," I said. "But it's still in its hiding place in my bedroom. She took *Manipulation of Magical Creatures — Big Creatures for Small Children*," I said, hoping against hope that this would not be as bad.

"Oh," said Violet dully. "That's probably worse."

20

Deceit, *noun* misrepresentation; sometimes necessary when telling the truth could lead to big complications, but can leave a lingering feeling of doubt and guilt once employed.

Violet came over to our house uncharacteristically early the following morning. She was determined to get the book back. She scoffed at my suggestion that some form of magic could be used to retrieve it.

"It's a book of spells, Anna," she said condescendingly. "Spell books are protected by magic," she explained. "You need a magical permit or licence to buy them and there are spells protecting their movement."

"Not very effective spells," I huffed. "I mean if Rita Raton managed to break into your house and take it without any magic, there's a problem."

"Yes," Violet pondered. "You've got a point. The problem with a lot of protection spells is that they are designed to protect things against magic. No one's really thinking about protecting books like that from non-magical creatures. But then again I suppose it's because there aren't supposed to be spell books in the non-magical world. It means that someone like Rita Raton can walk into the house and steal a book of spells but we can't use magic to get it back. The book itself is magic-resistant."

"Magic-resistant?" I said, thinking it sounded ridiculous that a book of magic spells could be magic-resistant.

"Yes, magic-resistant," said Violet. "Think of it like magical waterproofing. You know how water runs off plastic raincoats and umbrellas?" She spoke the word "plastic" with reverence and respect.

"Magical waterproofing?" I asked.

"Correct," said Violet, dragging her mind away from the wonders of plastic with obvious effort. "Well, magic spells aimed at a spell book run off them, like water runs off an umbrella."

"Okay," I said slowly, trying to digest the concept.

"Remember when we were trying to find the spell book in the first place, to summon Charlene?" she said. "I wouldn't have gotten you, Tabitha and Greta to help me hunt for it if I'd been able to use a finding spell to find it."

I tried not to think about how Violet used me in the summoning of Charlene and considered what Violet was saying.

"What about when your mum gave me *Torture and Torment?*" I asked. "She summoned it and it appeared."

"*Torture and Torment — Everything You Need to Know About the Persecution of Creatures of Magic, Children's Edition, Volume One* is a history textbook, Anna," Violet explained. "It's not magic."

I understood.

"So if you can't click your fingers and get the spell book back, how are you going to get it?" I asked.

"We are going to go to Rita Raton's house and steal it back," said Violet. "I have a plan."

I knew where the Ratons lived. Rita Raton had left her name and address with Mum. "In case anything comes up and you want to contact me," she had said.

All the same, I wasn't entirely comfortable with Violet's plan. While I respected the need to retrieve *Manipulation of Magical Creatures — Big Creatures for Small People,* I didn't see why a more straightforward method couldn't be used, a method involving parental support or at least partial parental support. (Getting Mum to drive us to the Ratons' house was a good way to go in my mind.)

Her plan involved the classic reverse sleepover. A reverse sleepover is when you tell your parents you are sleeping over at a friend's house, and the friend tells her parents that she is sleeping over at your house. This only really works if you have parents that don't call to confirm the sleepover arrangements. I'd seen teenagers do this on an old American movie I'd watched one Sunday afternoon, so I knew what Violet was talking about. I think the movie was made in the days before mobile phones and texting as these things made checking on your children quick and easy. I felt very uncomfortable with the whole idea, but Violet managed to talk me round.

Unlike me, Violet was confident our parents wouldn't check with each other and felt completely comfortable deceiving them. We'd already had a couple of sleepovers at each other's houses and Violet thought if we treated it really casually, it would be okay.

I didn't think it would work for a number of reasons:

1. If I was too casual about mentioning a sleepover, my mother would smell a rat.

2. My mother was a lot stricter in general than Pamela, and I thought it unlikely she wouldn't contact Pamela to check.

3. I didn't like lying to my parents and I was an unconvincing liar.

Mum did call Pamela to check that it was okay if I slept over at the Browns but luckily she spoke to Violet's father, who was vague at the best of times. I was at Violet's house when

Mum called and I could hear John Brown saying, "Yes, yes, not a problem. Yes, that's right. I have a function over there. No, it's no problem to take the girls."

When he got off the phone he said, "So you're coming here for a sleepover tonight, Greta." (He always got Greta and my names confused, even though we looked nothing alike, and Mum had confirmed that it was me who was sleeping over.)

Violet took over smoothly.

"Oh, Father," she said. "No, it's me going over to Anna's house, you must have misheard Dorothy."

"Could you call me Dad?" asked John Brown. "Dad, I am going over to Anna's house?"

"Dad, I am going over to Anna's house," Violet repeated obediently.

"If you say so," said John Brown. "I know I'm taking the other girls to Guide Camp. If you want to go over to Anna's house, that's fine." He was going upstairs to talk to Charlene. Since work on the swimming pool had begun they were making a greater effort to get along. Charlene had shared some insights about musical technique and how to make an impact on an audience, and John had apparently put her advice to good use and was keen to learn more.

We had packed our bags earlier that afternoon. Rita Raton

lived in the same city as we did, but in one of its outer suburbs, surrounded by national park. Violet's idea was that we break into their house at night and then sleep in the national park after finding the book. In spite of the heat we packed sleeping-bags, just in case. Violet had also packed some snacks and water and two torches.

Pamela was watching a DVD of her favourite TV show. It was an old one called *Bewitched*. It featured a woman called Samantha who was a witch pretending to be an ordinary woman. She even had a daughter called Tabitha, just like Pamela.

"Mother, I'm going next door to Anna's for my sleepover," said Violet. "Father's already spoken to Dorothy."

"Okay, have fun," said Pamela, absently kissing Violet on the cheek. She was engrossed in her show.

And that's how we found ourselves walking to the train station on our book-stealing mission on a hot afternoon in January.

21

Disaster, *noun* **when things suddenly go terribly wrong on a calamitous scale.**

T he first part of the trip went smoothly enough.

We agreed that we would wait until the Ratons were asleep before we went into the house. Violet said that she was very good at darkness enhancement, which she explained meant she could make the night seem darker than it really was to help conceal us. This would be necessary as it was close to a full moon and the nights had been bright.

We caught the train from our local station into the city, and changed trains for the suburb where the Ratons lived. Violet had printed out a picture of the Ratons' house from Google Earth. It was a fair walk from the closest station and we planned to take a short cut through the national park that curled around the back of their property.

It was a good idea in theory. Unfortunately, we had to get off the train a few stops early because of track work on the railway line. The bus ride seemed to take forever and we ate most of our snacks while we played I-spy. It wasn't a successful game. Although you play I-spy mostly in a car or on a train, it isn't a game suited to journeys because what you spy one minute is gone the next. This makes it difficult for the other person to guess what you spied. After a particularly tedious round, I gave up trying to guess what Violet had spied (it was a dead flying fox on a power line that we had passed ten minutes before). Just then, we realised that the bus had pulled up at the Ratons' train station. We had to rush from our seats at the back of the bus to get off in time and then realised we'd left our sleeping-bags and umbrella behind.

It was at this point we became irritable with one another. I was already slightly irritated with Violet because I thought the flying fox was an unfair choice for I-spy, and I was irritated with myself because I knew a game of I-spy was a stupid thing to be irritated about. We both blamed playing I-spy for our leaving the sleeping-bags on the bus. Violet said if I hadn't been so slow to guess that something beginning with "f" could only be a flying fox, we wouldn't have left the bus in such a rush. I told Violet that just because she had a cat-like obsession with rat-like animals she shouldn't expect everyone else to notice them.

We were walking along the track into the national park as we had this argument, not concentrating on where we were going. The tree shadows were starting to join together. I checked my watch — it was eight o'clock. Violet stopped dead in her tracks and motioned for me to do the same.

"Did you hear that?" she whispered.

I listened. I heard leaves crackling underfoot but the sound seemed to stop when we stopped.

"Not really," I whispered back.

"What do you mean, not really?" asked Violet, still sounding irritated. "Either you heard something or you didn't."

"I thought I could hear the sound of someone behind us," I whispered. "But it seems to have stopped now."

We both listened. It had suddenly become a lot darker. The sun was going down and it was difficult to see too far behind or ahead of us. Our torches had been in the same bag as the sleeping-bags — the sleeping-bags that we had left on the bus.

"I think someone is following us," Violet whispered.

Cautiously, we started to walk again. I realised Violet was right. When we walked, I could hear the faint sound of dry leaves and twigs crackling underfoot behind us. When we stopped, the sound stopped. And when we turned around there was no one there.

I shivered. It was getting dark, we had no torches, we were in the middle of bushland and my parents had no idea where I was. I was glad to feel Violet's hand reaching for mine.

"How far do you think we have to go?" I asked quietly.

Violet looked down at the map.

"How can you possibly read that?" I asked, amazed. The darkness had really thickened now.

"Even when I'm not in cat form I have excellent night vision," Violet said. "We probably have another fifteen minutes of walking, but we're going to have to leave this track soon and climb across that rocky bit to get to the back of the Ratons' house."

I peered ahead. The track, as Violet described it, was very faint. I wouldn't have been able to follow it without the assistance of her night vision. I could vaguely make out some boulders at the top of a hill.

I didn't want to think about what could be behind us. Animal or human — it was an equally scary prospect. Scarier still would be something that was neither human or animal. I desperately hoped that what we were hearing were native animals, curious about what two girls were doing, walking through their bushland at night, and not magical monsters.

You might notice that I've referred to "animals" and

"monsters" plural. That was the other thing I had noticed about the footsteps following us: there were two sets of them, not one. Whatever was following us had brought a friend.

❀

We had left the track and were starting to climb over the rocks when the rain started. It was sudden, tropical summer rain and it was heavy. It didn't take long before we were both soaking wet. Violet looked like she wanted to hiss.

"Cursed rain," she said through gritted teeth. "Hope for the best but prepare for the worst."

I knew she was thinking about the umbrella we had left on the bus with our sleeping-bags.

Slippery moss-covered boulders combined with the dark made climbing difficult. I thought of Greta and her talent for climbing and wished I was more like my sister. Violet was ahead of me, her night vision making it easier for her to find a path through the rocks.

I tripped on a rock and slid down one of the boulders, scraping the underside of my legs. My foot caught between two small rocks and twisted as I landed. I felt excruciating pain.

"Violet," I sobbed. "Violet, I've done something to my foot."

Violet was back in a flash. She kneeled down and delicately moved the rocks from either side of my foot.

I gasped and tried to breathe. There was room for nothing in my mind but the pain.

Violet looked at me, scared. I could tell she was thinking hard.

"Anna, I'm going to have to do some magic," she said softly. "It could draw attention to us, but this is an emergency. Don't be scared; I need you to trust me for this to work."

She started to fiddle with her cat brooch and before I realised what she was doing she handed it to me.

"Anna, this will help keep you safe."

I nodded. The emblem felt cold and hard in my hand. I couldn't speak because of the pain but I knew Violet had just given me her most valuable possession.

Violet drew her hands together, singing in a low voice. I couldn't understand the words; it wasn't a language I understood. She slowly moved her arms backwards and the rain that was falling around us drew back until we were sitting in a cocoon of dryness. It was like being in a house with invisible walls while the rain fell outside.

Violet took my foot in her hands. She started to sing again, a cross between humming and crooning, and as she touched my foot the pain began to subside. It was such a relief. It took me a few seconds to realise that along with the departure of pain, all feeling in my foot had gone. It felt like I no longer *had* a foot. Experimentally, I tapped my ankle. I couldn't feel a thing. I tapped my calf, which I could feel. It was only below my ankle that all sensation had vanished, as though someone had drawn an invisible line around the top of my ankle and for feeling purposes it had ceased to exist. My foot looked strange. It was red and swollen.

I could see Violet examining my foot as well. She was worried. I felt worried that she was worried.

I tried to stand up, but I couldn't put any weight on my injured foot.

"Violet, I can't walk," I said.

"I know," she said.

I suddenly realised why she had given me the emblem. "Violet, are you leaving me here?" I asked in a small voice. "Alone? Violet, please don't leave me here."

Violet looked unhappy but determined.

"Anna, I don't have a choice. Your foot is hurt, badly hurt, and what I've done to numb it won't last more than a couple of hours. You need to go to hospital. Trust me."

That was part of the problem. I wasn't sure I did. I felt the cold metal of the emblem in my hand.

"But what about the book?" I asked.

"Forget the book," said Violet, wearily. "We'll work something else out with the book."

I knew what it must have cost Violet to say that. If she meant it – getting the book back was so important to her. There was a lump in my throat. I had mucked everything up by tripping over that stupid rock. Violet gave me a hug. She was not a hugging kind of person and she felt a bit stiff but she was trying. Having her try made the lump in my throat grow bigger and as the tears trickled down my cheeks she looked away. Violet was thoughtful like that. She was a person who respected privacy. Or someone who found it difficult to deal with emotion. I cried more.

Violet stopped hugging me.

"I'm sorry, Anna, but you're making my T-shirt even wetter." She gave a shudder and I started to laugh even though I was still crying.

"Anna, I have to depart," Violet said. She unwrapped the silver elastic bracelet from her wrist and wrapped it around mine. "I'll make sure nothing can hurt you. I'm just going to have to step outside." She braced herself and walked out into the rain.

Waving her arms about again, she started humming and then tapped in front of her. Although it looked like she was tapping air there was a sound like she was knocking on glass, invisible glass. I leaned over and felt in front of me. A smooth, invisible wall extended about an arm's length around and above me. It was snug without being claustrophobic.

"No one will be able to come in and get you until I come back," Violet said. She didn't mention the sounds we had heard behind us, but I knew that's what she was thinking about.

"Do you think you could give me some light?" I asked in a small voice.

Violet sighed. "If you wish. But it won't help your night vision, you know." She hummed and tapped the invisible glass and it lit up with a soft golden glow.

It was like I was trapped in a low wattage light globe. I realised what Violet meant about my night vision. Even though everything inside my haven was dry and light, when I looked out into the bush the night was even darker than before. I was blinded by the light in my little room. I couldn't see Violet and struggled to focus my eyes on where she had been standing. As my eyes slowly adjusted I realised Violet had disappeared. My heart flip-flopped. Had she left me already? Squinting out of my glass cocoon I realised there was a small black cat crouched outside. The cat was completely black, which made her even more difficult to spot in the darkness. Her eyes glowed green. She stared at me with Violet's eyes.

"Violet?" I asked hesitantly.

"Meow," said the cat, looking at me with an intelligent expression on her whiskered face.

It made sense. Violet would be able to travel more quickly in cat form, and her night vision would become more acute. But I was worried. Violet had said that she was a target when she was a cat because she was so obviously a Creature of Magic with her completely black coat. She was running a huge risk changing form, especially when we were so close to the Ratons' house. Who knew what other Inquisitors were living in the area? And didn't she need to wear her emblem? I was no longer worried about my ankle, or being alone in the bush at night, or being followed by who knew what kind of scary creatures. Violet was putting herself in danger for me, and I wanted her to be safe.

"Run, Violet, run!" I urged. "I'll be fine!"

With a flick of her elegant tail she was gone. I watched until she disappeared into the silky summer night.

22

Sister, *noun* female sibling; member of your family
who is often extremely annoying but sometimes
surprises you with her behaviour; someone you love.

My bravado lasted for two whole minutes. I timed myself on my watch. It was difficult to continue being brave alone and injured in the middle of bushland at night.

I was acutely aware that while I couldn't see out into the night, the light inside my little room meant that whatever was out there could see in very easily. I may as well have had a big arrow pointing directly at me. This would be good if Violet brought help, but bad if other people or creatures with less wholesome intentions were searching for me.

Now that Violet was gone and there was no conversation to distract me I became sensitive to every sound. There were small rustling noises, like animals scuffling through the undergrowth, and I heard the occasional shriek of an owl. These sounds didn't really scare me. I knew what they were and they belonged in the bush.

What did scare me was the sound of the footsteps. They had started again not long after Violet left. At first they were faint but they started to get a lot closer. Occasionally, I thought I heard voices whispering as well. I was terrified. I kept tapping the invisible glass around me to make sure it was still there, that I was still safe. I tested every millimetre around me to ensure that there were no gaps in my invisible cocoon.

To try to distract myself, I thought about what everyone at home was doing. It was after nine o'clock. Mum and Dad would be sitting on the couch, watching the cricket. My eyes prickled with tears. No one even knew I was missing.

The sound of the footsteps was getting louder. The whispering had stopped and I could hear feet climbing over the boulders. I tried very hard to think brave thoughts. There was no way whatever was out there could get into my glass cocoon. But my heart was beating wildly. It is not very comforting being protected by an invisible wall.

The whispering began again and I could see something flickering in the boulders. Whatever was out there was getting very close, and had a torch, or eyes that looked like a torch. I kept as still as I could, regretting asking Violet to make a light for me.

The sound of crunching undergrowth stopped. My pursuers were finally standing directly outside my cocoon. I couldn't make out their figures. They were shining their torches directly into my face, which I hid in my hands, instinctively regressing to the childlike thinking that if I couldn't see them, maybe they couldn't see me.

Then the last voice I expected to hear asked, "Anna, is that you?"

"Greta!" I cried, looking up. I could just make out her face.

"I'm here too," said Tabitha, putting her torch down and moving towards me, hitting her head on the invisible glass. "Ouch, what is that stuff?" She felt the air in front of her, placing her hands flat on the invisible wall, feeling her way along.

"Is there any way in?" she asked.

"Not that I know of," I said. "Our aim was to keep people out. I wouldn't be able to get out myself, even if I could move."

"What's wrong with you, Anna?" asked Greta, sitting down cross-legged, as though it was the most natural thing in the world to find her sister enclosed in an invisible glass cocoon in the middle of a national park, a long way from home at night. "Have you hurt yourself?"

"I got my stupid foot caught between some rocks," I said

ruefully. "I think it's broken or at least badly sprained. Violet has gone for help."

"Bum," Greta said. "Does it hurt?"

"Not so much since Violet worked some magic on it," I said. "But what are you doing here? How did you know where we were?"

"You and Violet have been up to something for days, and I saw you getting the sleeping-bags out of the shed," said Greta. "Tabitha did some spy work about where you were going and came up with Rita Raton and her address."

Tabitha verified this. "Yes, I did a bit of listening at the door. Your voice can be loud, Anna, and I always know where you are because of the way you slam doors. Even when you think you are whispering you're easy to hear. And you said you were going through bushland behind Rita's house."

"I used Google maps," said Greta. "On my iPad." She glanced at her watch. "21.30 hours. Not a bad time for a two-kilometre trek, even with the wildlife observation break."

"But how did you get here?" I asked.

Tabitha looked at me. "Dad drove us."

It was so simple. But it worked. I felt proud of my sister. She could be so annoying, but she was unbelievable.

My head was spinning.

"So won't Mum be looking for you?"

Greta said patiently, "Mum, John and Pamela think we're at Guide Camp. John dropped us here. He had a function he was playing at nearby and Mum had already arranged for him to drop us at the camp. We mucked around and John was running late so we said to drop us outside the gate and he did. We went cross-country from there. It took us a while to track you down, and we wanted to make sure it was you before we made contact. And we found some marsupial mice. Tabs caught one."

"I didn't hurt it," Tabitha was quick to add. "They were sooo cute. They looked a bit like Fuzzy, only bigger and they were fast. Greta wanted to have a closer look so I caught one but it took ages, I had to—"

"We lost you when Tabs was catching the mouse, but we could see the light from your cage," explained Greta. "So what now, Anna? What's the deal with Rita Raton?"

"Are you looking for something?" Tabitha asked.

Greta must have read my thoughts. "Tabitha's my friend, Anna. She does tell me stuff, probably more stuff than Violet tells you."

"I don't think so," I said.

"Greta knows about the Inquisitoriers," Tabitha chimed in. "And she knows about us being Creatures of Magic."

Tabitha was a chatterbox. She probably *had* told Greta more stuff than Violet had told me, just because she talked so much.

"What do you know about Rita Raton?" I asked Tabitha.

"What about her?" Tabitha asked. "I know she's bad, and pretty high up in the Inquisithingies, and Arthur Raton is bad, clever and bad. Most Inquisithingies are pretty stupid but not Arthur. I know we moved into their old house."

"Why did you do that?" I asked. It was something that had been bothering me. Moving into your arch enemy's house didn't seem like a good way to avoid them. "And maybe you're thinking of the wrong Ratons. There was no Arthur."

"There is only one set of Ratons," Tabitha said. "Mum thought that at least we could be sure they wouldn't be living around the corner if we moved into their old place. She knew they were moving a fair way away and thought their old house would be the last place Rita Raton would expect any Creature of Magic to turn up."

"Mmm," I said. It sounded like typical Pamela logic, a bit wacky but possibly containing some small amount of merit. "Did you know that Rita Raton broke into your house while you were away and stole a book of spells?"

"Oh, naaasty," drawled Tabitha. "No, I didn't know that. Mum would have kittens if she knew that. If she hadn't already had them, which she has of course, you do know—" she added.

"Yes, I know about all that," I interrupted, not wanting Tabitha to start some longwinded explanation about the Browns' feline transformation abilities. "Violet and I were on our way to Rita's house to steal the book back when I hurt my ankle," I continued. "We're not very far away from their house. I think their backyard starts when the rocky bit here finishes."

Tabitha and Greta looked at each other.

"Are you thinking what I'm thinking, Tabs?" Greta asked Tabitha.

"Maybe I am, Grets," Tabitha replied.

They turned to me.

"Would you be okay, Anna, if we left you here and went to the Ratons' house to steal the book?" Greta asked.

"What was the name of the book?" Tabitha asked.

I looked at them sitting there so seriously. I didn't want Greta to steal the book back. I wanted to be the one to get the book. It was my and Violet's mission, not Greta and Tabitha's.

"You can't find the book," I said.

"Why not?" asked Greta. "We found you."

She had a point. Why couldn't they find the book? Getting it back was the important thing, not who did it. It was mean for me not to want them to do it just because I wanted the glory myself. I made up my mind.

"It's that book of spells we used to summon Charlene," I said. "And you already know their address."

Tabitha and Greta jumped up, their eyes shining.

"We'll come back as soon as we've got the book, Anna, I promise," Greta said with excitement.

"Be careful!" I said. But they were already gone, nimbly making their way through the rocks, chattering like birds. I was alone again.

I wasn't as scared now that I couldn't hear some unknown being making its way towards me. I was more worried for Violet, Greta and Tabitha than myself. I wondered who Violet would go to for help. Police? Helicopter ambulance? Pamela? Violet would have a lot of explaining to do. She would hate letting the cat out of the bag. I decided she'd go to Pamela.

What was I going to tell Mum and Dad? They were going to be so angry with me. Well, they'd probably be upset and worried because of my ankle first, but once they knew that was going to be all right they would be really cross. Faking a sleepover at Violet's, catching buses and trains and trekking through bushland at night would be enough to make me a juvenile delinquent in their minds. I would probably be grounded for the next ten years. In the middle of these gloomy thoughts I noticed the now familiar sound of footsteps treading lightly over the rocks.

I brightened. Hopefully this was help sent by Violet. I would have preferred a helicopter, but I would settle for anybody at this stage. Anybody good, at least.

A tall shadowy figure emerged from the rocks and came up to the side of my glass cocoon.

"Anna?" Pamela asked in surprise. "Anna is that you? What are you doing in there?"

She felt the glass just like Tabitha had done.

"What are you doing in an invisible glass cage?" she asked.

I rolled my eyes. "Didn't Violet tell you what happened? I think I've broken my ankle," I said.

Pamela looked puzzled.

"Where's Violet?" she asked. "Don't tell me I've lost another child! I'm looking for Tabs. She left a map of the national park and an address in her room — John said she'd gone to Guide Camp with Greta, but Dorothy knew nothing about it. It smelled fishy. I called the camp and she wasn't there. What's up with you children?"

I kept quiet. I knew she wasn't looking for a proper answer.

Pamela continued, "All very, very fishy — when she wasn't

at the camp I thought it best not to make a fuss so I told the Guide Camp I'd had made a mistake about Tabitha, that I had forgotten she was with my husband."

"They must have thought you were a bit strange," I said, imagining the conversation.

"They're not the first," said Pamela matter-of-factly.

"But what about Violet — isn't she with you?" I asked, trying to work out what had happened.

"I haven't seen Violet since this afternoon," Pamela explained.

The implications of what Pamela was saying began to sink in.

"Violet was here with me, Pamela. She changed into cat form to get help for me, or at least that's what she told me," I said. "She left me her cat brooch. I thought she must have told you I was in trouble."

Pamela's eyes widened when she saw Violet's brooch. "No," she said slowly. "I haven't seen Violet. I didn't know she was missing."

I decided to tell Pamela what I knew. Either Violet had lied to me about going for help or she was in trouble. This was serious.

"Tabitha was just here with Greta."

"But Greta is at Guide Camp," Pamela said.

"No, she's not. I don't have time to explain, Pamela. The important thing is where they have gone."

"Yes, I know where Tabitha has gone," Pamela said. "She's gone to Wollemi Street for some reason."

"Pamela, Rita Raton lives at Wollemi Street. Greta and Tabitha have gone to Rita Raton's house, and for all we know Violet could be there too. I'm worried about them, Pamela, really worried. Violet left here an hour and a half ago," I said, checking my watch.

"Rita Raton must have them. I hope Arthur isn't there," said Pamela with a tremor in her voice. Her hands clenched. "They're in trouble. And you have Violet's emblem."

23

Love, *verb* **when you will do anything to protect someone, with no consideration of the danger involved in doing so. Parents are often good at this.**

Pamela sat with her head in her hands. She was thinking hard. She eventually looked up.

"Why is everyone hunting Rita Raton, Anna?" she asked. "Do you know how dangerous that woman is and the lengths everyone has gone to, to keep our family safe from the Inquisitors? Do you know who Arthur Raton is?"

"No," I said, frustrated. "I do not know who Arthur Raton is, but I'd like to!"

"This is top secret, Anna," Pamela said seriously.

"I understand," I said.

Pamela looked over her shoulder to make sure no one was listening.

"Arthur Raton is Rita Raton's husband. He is the head of the Inquisitors and he is a cruel, vile and disgusting man —

he's wanted by the Bureau for crimes against Creatures but he's been in hiding for some time. I don't even know when Rita Raton last saw him. But, Anna, I don't understand why all of you children are trying to find Rita Raton. She is not as dangerous as Arthur but she is still dangerous, particularly to Violet and Tabitha."

It was my turn to explain.

"Pamela, do you know what Rita did when she visited us?"

Pamela shook her head.

I described Rita Raton's visit to our house with Edward and Emily, and how Edward and Emily had only received a letter from Santa Claus. I explained how Rita Raton had broken into Pamela's house and stolen the book, and Violet's distress and our mission to get it back. I told her how Greta and Tabitha had followed us and how they had now gone to get the book. I added that I hadn't really wanted to come out to the national park, that I had wanted to tell our parents, but that Violet had been very clear that this was a bad idea (this was a dibber-dobberish thing to say, I know, and not very loyal to Violet, but I was too tired to dress up the truth). By the time I had finished, Pamela was starting to look angry.

It wasn't something I had seen before. She had been annoyed about the mermaid and was sometimes irritated by Brendan and

Orlando's mucking around, but she wasn't a person who was angry very often. She looked scary.

"How bad is your ankle?" she asked.

"Pretty bad," I said. "Violet did something to stop it hurting, but I can't walk on it." I was worried that Pamela would leave me behind like Violet, Tabitha and Greta had done, safe but bored in my invisible industrial-strength glass cocoon.

I needn't have worried. Not about being left behind anyway.

Pamela sprang into action. She rubbed her hands gently against the walls of my cocoon, hummed softly and then snapped her fingers. There was the sound of shattering glass shards bouncing off the rocks around us. I tried to stand up.

"Careful," said Pamela, sharply. "Just because you can't see the glass doesn't mean that it can't cut you."

She hummed again and waved her arms like a conductor in front of an orchestra. I could hear the glass shards being swept into a pile. Pamela snapped her fingers and glass tinkled against glass, breaking into a million tiny pieces. She built a pyramid of rocks on top of the glass, then she looked at my ankle.

She examined it carefully, moving it this way and that. I still couldn't feel anything and it was starting to turn purple.

"You do know about the whole cat thing, Anna?" she asked.

I nodded. Pamela looked at me in an appraising way.

"We need to go and sort out this nonsense about the book. We are going to find Violet, Tabitha and Greta and take them home."

"Yes," I said. Pamela was stating the obvious but she was still looking angry, and I didn't want to say much. She had said "we" when she spoke about finding the girls and the book. Was my part in this adventure about to become more active?

"Can I come too, Pamela?" I asked uncertainly. "I mean I'd love to but I can't walk."

Pamela stared at me with her green cat's eyes.

"Do you trust me, Anna?" she asked. "I need to work some magic so you can come with me, but you need to trust me and understand that what I am about to do will not harm you, not in a permanent way."

"I trust you, Pamela," I said. I knew whatever was about to happen was serious. And it was true – I did trust her.

Pamela carefully unpinned her cat brooch and attached it to the silver leather bracelet around her wrist.

"I need you to close your eyes and remain completely still and quiet," Pamela said. "It shouldn't take too long, and don't be scared. I won't let anything bad happen to you. I mean, you do like cats, don't you?"

I didn't answer as I thought it might be a trick question — she had told me to remain completely quiet. I stood still and closed my eyes. I could hear Pamela humming and singing alternately and I became aware of a strange sensation creeping over me. It felt like my feet were shrinking up into my legs and my hands into my arms. My clothes seemed to be shrinking with me, eventually becoming so light I could no longer feel them. My skin began to feel prickly. Goosebumps spread across my skin: big goosebumps, ganderbumps. Little stalks of something were growing out of the goosebumps. I was sprouting fur! Pamela told me to open my eyes, although she didn't speak aloud. A feeling, rather than a voice, compelled me to look. So I did. And what I saw was the strangest thing I have ever seen in my life.

Pamela had completely disappeared and in her place stood a majestic calico cat with white whiskers, wearing a silver leather collar with her emblem dangling next to the small silver bell. She had patches of black, gold and brown over her predominantly white coat and tawny green eyes. Either she was an enormous cat or I had shrunk because I was looking up to her rather than down. It was when I looked down that I realised what had happened to me. There were two ginger paws where my legs should have been.

Pamela had changed me into a cat.

I flicked my tail. It was a nice if strange sensation. Although the light from my cocoon had gone I could see just as clearly, in fact probably more clearly. As a cat I did not need glasses, or had my glasses become part of me? And the sounds. There were sounds everywhere, of small animals scuttling, tiny pieces of bark breaking and even some faint human voices in the distance. And smells. I could smell the lemon scented gums through the rain and the harsher eucalyptus smell of the gum trees towering above me. I stepped forwards experimentally on my four paws and heard the tinkle of a small bell. I was wearing Violet's collar and I could feel the weight of Violet's emblem attached to it. I took another step, feeling the rocks between my padded feet. It felt a bit like walking with thick socks on. The pain in my ankle was gone.

Pamela flicked her tail and gave a low meow. It wasn't like the meow could be directly translated into words, but I somehow knew that it meant to get going and follow her which I did. She quickly walked over the boulders which were so much easier to climb with my four cat paws rather than my human two legs. Looking back I can't remember feeling especially surprised. It was as though all my human emotions had dissolved when I became a cat, so my feelings were now cat based rather than human. I wasn't surprised to be a cat because I was a cat.

It didn't take us long to reach the Ratons' house. I became very excited by a bush mouse that crossed our path, and momentarily forgot our mission with the thrill of the chase. Pamela quickly pulled me into line. I felt grateful she did. I don't know whether I could have lived with myself if I had caught the mouse. I mean what would I have done with it? Eaten it?

The bush became less bushy and the friendly busy sounds in it were being replaced by the more hostile sounds of the suburbs. I heard the faint sound of cars travelling up the highway and trains rattling in the distance. I saw lights that must have belonged to houses (not many because it was past midnight) and streetlights as well.

There were different smells too. There was a nice kind of meaty smell left over from a barbecue earlier in the night and another smell that was a bit scary. The scary smell seemed to get closer as we reached the Ratons' house to the point where I didn't want to go any further. I could feel the fur on my tail starting to stick out and before I knew what I was doing a low growl escaped from my throat. Pamela turned around to look at me. I knew she was telling me to keep on moving and to be quiet so I did, but I was fighting an instinct that was telling me very strongly to turn back, and the closer I got to Rita Raton's house the stronger my fear became.

I froze at the sudden sound of a dog barking. We had just crawled under Rita Raton's front fence — there was a number on the gate that confirmed it was the right house, but I don't think we read this. At least I certainly didn't. As a cat I couldn't read; maybe Pamela as a magical cat could. We were operating by instinct. I knew that this was the Ratons' house, although I can't now explain why. It was a combination of smells and feelings, as well as Pamela leading me on.

The dog barked again and I heard the pitter-pattering of dog paws down the driveway towards me. The fur on my back and tail was fully upright and I can remember being tense with fear.

Even Pamela stopped in her tracks as the corgi approached us. He was growling and his teeth were bared. He walked up to Pamela first as she was closer, or maybe it was because he sensed that she was the greater threat. Pamela growled. It was a growl that came from deep in her throat and while it wasn't very loud, it was full of menace and the promise of pain. The dog stopped. Pamela growled again and hissed. As the dog tentatively took a step closer Pamela reached out one majestic calico paw and swiped it across the nose. It was a swipe with bite; she must have had her claws bared.

The dog ran yelping towards the backyard and Pamela turned to me. I knew she wanted me to follow her. Silently, we padded to the house. At first glance there were no lights, suggesting everyone was asleep. My cat brain registered no movement around the house, but some instinct told me there was danger. Not the obvious threat of dog towards cat, but a more subtle, poisonous kind of danger that filled me with dread.

Pamela had stopped as well. I knew she could feel it too and we both sat for a moment, sniffing the air. If I had been thinking as Anna rather than a cat, I would have wondered where Greta and Tabitha were. Surely they must have made it to the house by now? It was unnaturally quiet.

Pamela started to walk around to the back of the house, and I could tell by the angle of her tail she was in a state of extreme alertness. The house was built into the slope of a hill and there was a big rumpus room on the lower ground level at the back. There was no light on, but the light of the moon and our night vision made what was inside visible. And what we saw was enough to send a chill through our hearts.

In the middle of the room was a large cage. Two corgis paced back and forth in front of it, growling. Nearby a hooded figure was hunched over a glowing green-screened computer.

The fur on my back stood up when I saw what was in the cage.

Tabitha and Greta were huddled together with a small black cat crouched at their feet. Their hands and feet were tied and a sudden beam of moonlight illuminated their tear-stained, terrified faces.

24

Rescue, *verb* **to free from danger.**

I could feel Pamela's emotion. She rushed at the door, meowing, and tried to open the sliding doors with her paws, but she didn't have the strength. She ran frustrated back and forth across the length of the door, yowling with rage. Then she stopped and stood still and seemed to be thinking. It was as though she had remembered she wasn't really a cat but a human and could reason things through rather than rely solely on instinct. She seemed to become positively swollen with thought and then I realised she *was* growing. As I watched she became taller and wider until she was the size of a small lion.

The figure at the computer looked up, alarm registering on her face. Rita Raton. She rushed towards the door to make sure it was locked and then drew the curtains across the sliding doors. I don't know what she was thinking. Was she hoping that if she couldn't see the giant cat outside her back door that it would magically disappear?

Because of the closed curtains Rita Raton didn't get to see what Pamela did next, which was truly scary. I was scared and I was Pamela's friend, so as her enemy I knew that Rita would be rightly petrified. Enemy is a strong word, but I knew the gravity of the situation from the moment we saw the children in the cage. I knew Pamela was very, very angry and although I had only known Creatures of Magic to be benevolent, I had a feeling that my lighthearted view of magic was about to change. Every strand of fur on my body was raised.

Pamela began to morph back from cat to human. It was like watching a horror movie. It probably only took a minute but it was a very long minute. At one stage she was part giant cat and part human. A giant cat with an angry human face is not a pretty sight. As Pamela's fur receded her clothes resurfaced on her body, partly ripped and very grubby. They told the tale of our journey through the national park — they were covered in dirt and had bits of grass and dead leaves clinging to them. The only constant was Pamela's emblem, which she quickly unhooked from the silver leather cat's collar and repinned to her ripped shirt. She wrapped the collar around her wrist. Now that I recognised what it was, it was difficult to understand how I had failed to do so before — the bracelet she always wore was a cat's collar.

I wondered briefly how she was going to get into the room.

She pulled at the sliding door but it was locked. With a stern face she raised her arms together and started to hum. There was static in the air — some kind of electrical force — and as Pamela's arms dropped down the entire glass door shattered, just like my invisible glass cocoon had shattered on her command.

The corgis charged through the broken door with their teeth bared and leaped towards Pamela's throat. She didn't flinch. She raised her arms again and it was as though the dogs became puppets, manipulated with invisible strings. They rocked gently through the air and landed at Rita Raton's feet, unhurt but clearly shaken. They whimpered, looking to Rita Raton for comfort. She ignored them and scuttled over to the cage where Tabitha and Greta were cowering.

Pamela marched up to the cage, throwing her arms around and flinging words like missiles. There was no gentle humming now. The cage exploded. A whirlpool of metal bars whizzed around the room with lethal force. Rita ducked to avoid being hit on the head. The dogs whimpered and crept further under the desk, and even Greta and Tabitha ducked to avoid the flying metal bars. The only creature in the room seemingly unfazed by the explosion of the cage was the little black cat, who pressed her belly close to the floor and crawled across the carpet, looking at me as she went. She was telling me to follow her. It was funny, I think it must have been because I was myself a cat that I didn't think to stay and check on Greta or Tabitha or even what was happening between Pamela and Rita Raton. My cat mind knew I had to follow Violet so I did.

We made our way up the stairs and I suddenly realised I was being followed by cats, several cats in fact. It seemed like every cat from the suburb knew there was something serious happening and had come to help their part-feline friends.

Violet led us up the stairs and into various rooms. She was looking for something, which she found in Rita Raton's bedroom. It was *Manipulation of Magical Creatures*. She pulled it off Rita's bedside table with her paws, then apparently came to the conclusion that the rescue of the book would be better achieved in human rather than cat form.

As a matter of natural cat courtesy I turned away and looked around Rita's bedroom. It was a creepy room to be in as a cat and I think I would have found it creepy as a human as well. There were two large display cabinets, one eerily similar to the cabinet the Browns had in their study. But instead of taxidermic rodents there were cats — taxidermic cats. They had obviously died unhappy deaths — there were no purring cats curled up as though they were sleeping by the fire — they looked scared and angry. Some were crouched down in a growling pose and some were standing with the fur on their backs upright. I shivered. The cats were all wearing silver collars dangling with ornate bejewelled identity tags. I moved closer – the tags were emblems. The taxidermic cats were Creatures of Magic. I felt sick. What kind of person would do something like this?

The hate in the room was toxic. They wore emblems, so the killer must have known he was killing Creatures of Magic. My recent conversation with Pamela came back to me – I knew with a chilling certainty that this was the work of Arthur Raton. He had killed them, despite the magic of the emblems and the magic of the Creatures. The fur on my back rose.

The other cats hadn't entered the Ratons' bedroom. They probably obeyed an instinctual fear. They had wandered into the bedroom beside Rita's, and by the childlike sounds of delight coming from the bedroom they had met a warm welcome from Edward and Emily. I ran out Rita Raton's bedroom door and crouched in the hall outside. I couldn't get the image of the taxidermic cats out of my mind.

I felt my tension dissipate as someone started scratching me between the ears, which was a remarkably pleasant sensation. I rubbed up against the person's legs in pleasure. It was Violet. She bent down and gently traced a circle around my eyes.

"You are a pretty cat – your tabby markings look like your

glasses," she said. "It's unusual for girl cats to be ginger. You could be Ginger's sister." She removed the emblem from my collar and pinned it to her dirty white T-shirt. We looked at each other and I said an appreciative "thank you" meow to which Violet answered "you're welcome". I knew then once and for all that Violet did understand the language of cats. I anticipated her next move despite no words being spoken.

It was just as strange turning back into a human as it had been to turn into a cat. I felt myself growing and the room simultaneously becoming darker (I suppose I was losing my cat night vision). The goosebump sensation was inverted — it felt a bit like popping bubble wrap. The sensation covered my entire body as my cat fur folded back down into human skin and my clothes grew over me. Stunned, I looked down at my human legs and hands and tentatively tried to stand up on my two legs. I didn't succeed because the pain in my ankle returned.

Violet rushed over to support me.

"It feels a bit funny at first," said Violet. "You wonder exactly what you are. You can understand how Creatures of Magic have forgotten in the past."

I nodded and felt my glasses move up and down my nose. I wasn't sure whether my voice would work. I nodded again and felt suddenly teary. Violet held my hand and squeezed it.

I needed to see Greta and make sure she was all right. And I wanted to know what Pamela had done to Rita.

We checked in on Emily and Edward, Violet supporting me like a crutch. There were probably ten cats in the bedroom, jumping up on the beds and rolling over so Emily and Edward could tickle their stomachs and between their ears, a sensation I now understood the pleasure of. "Pwetty pussy!" Edward exclaimed in delight, patting the closest cat in the gentlest way his pudgy toddler hands could manage.

"Are you all right?" Violet asked Emily.

"This is fun," Emily said. She had two cats sitting in her lap and a third standing beside her. They were all purring.

I didn't need to tell Violet where I wanted to go — she knew. Together we made our way downstairs to the rumpus room.

25

Justice, *noun* when people
get what they deserve.

The scene that met us downstairs was truly magical. Two Christmas stockings, the biggest I had ever seen, sat on the floor. The names "Emily" and "Edward" were embroidered on them, and they were overflowing with toys. I could see a toy train in Edward's stocking and there was a small rabbit hutch beside Emily's. The was lots of chocolate, books with titles like *Misty Saves the Day*, *In Praise of Cats*, and *Glenda the Good White Witch to the Rescue*, giant stuffed toys, some bubble bath, a small tent, two scooters and some wonderful remote control mouse toys that squeaked as they moved and were incredibly lifelike. Tabitha and Greta were having a great time operating the mice with the remote controls, and some of the cats were joyfully chasing the mice around the room.

The cage had been reassembled and Rita was padlocked inside it. Three cats were standing guard and a fourth was sitting on the computer desk. It had a large key on its collar, which I guessed was the key to the cage. The violent corgis were nowhere to be seen and Pamela had calmed down.

She looked up as Violet and I came down the stairs and opened her arms wide to give Violet a big hug.

"Are you all right, kitten?" she asked.

Violet didn't say anything for a moment, snuggling into her mother.

"I'm recovering," she said. "And look, Mother, I've got the book."

Violet handed the book to Pamela.

"You know I care a lot more about you and Tabitha than some silly book," Pamela said. "We could have worked something out without you putting yourself in danger like this."

Violet didn't say anything. The strangest idea popped into my head. Did Violet want to get caught? After all, she wanted to go back to the Other Place . . .

I was distracted from these thoughts by the sound of Rita Raton's voice.

"How lovely," Rita sneered. "Witch and witch daughter reunited. Not for long once I get out of this cage and call the Bureau for Creatures of Magic! I'm sure they'll have a few things to say to you, Pamela Brown, about unlawful use of magic. You won't be allowed back into the non-magical community for some time, I'd say. There'll be a few years of exile for you because of this."

Pamela shot a withering look at Rita. "It's called the Bureau for the *Protection* of Creatures of Magic, Rita, and I think you're looking at a few breaches yourself. Don't worry, I'll be calling them myself to report on you. I can't believe they're not here already. Anyway, you can stay in the cage and wait for them unless you can convince the lovely Cleo to give you the key."

I guessed that Cleo was the pretty Australian spotted mist cat perched on the computer desk. She was watching the exchange between Pamela and Rita with intelligent green eyes. She began washing herself and the key jangled tantalisingly.

Rita growled, sounding like a cat herself.

Everyone ignored her.

"I suppose we should all make our way home," said Pamela, yawning and then looking surprised that she had done so. "Dear me, I really am acclimatising to this non-nocturnal life," she said. "Let's get home to bed. Now, Greta, what was this about Guide Camp? What time are you supposed to be home? Do you want to hide at our place until then? It might be a bit less complicated than explaining all these shenanigans to your parents. I think

215

there's going to be enough explaining to do around that ankle of Anna's without complicating the issue."

It was at that moment that Edward and Emily — flanked by a dozen cats — came down the stairs and ran towards the Christmas stockings. The children pulled out their presents with cries of delight. The flocking cats meowed with excitement as they saw the remote control mice.

"Santa Claus was delayed, children," Pamela said. "These are the presents that should have arrived on Christmas day."

In the midst of their happiness Emily and Edward stopped short when they saw their mother locked in a cage.

"Mother?" Emily said uncertainly, moving towards the cage.

Rita shrieked, "Get me the key and get away from those filthy, dirty cats! Edward! Stop touching the cats, you're allergic to them. DO NOT TOUCH THE CATS!"

I knew Rita did not like cats, but her reaction to her children being surrounded by them seemed extreme. And they certainly weren't displaying any symptoms of allergic reaction. If anything, it seemed to be the opposite. I had never seen Edward and Emily look so alive. Their cheeks were pink, their faces were animated and their green eyes were glowing. It was funny, I had never noticed their eyes before. They looked oddly familiar.

And then I realised.

They were cat's eyes, green eyes just like Violet's and Tabitha's and Pamela's.

"Have you ever played with cats before?" Pamela asked Emily gently.

Emily shook her head. "Mother has never let us," she said. "We're supposed to be allergic, but I don't feel sick touching them. They make me feel very happy. I almost feel like they are talking to me."

And that's when it happened. Two small ears poked up on Emily's head, and Edward scratched his bottom as a little black tail wavered up through the back of his pyjama pants. Rita's shrieking turned to loud theatrical crying, but the rest of us watched in wonder as Emily and Edward Raton transformed into black kittens.

"They're Creatures of Magic," said Pamela, reverently. "I did wonder."

"They're just like me," said Violet in a whisper.

"Only they haven't found their real mother yet," said Pamela, scratching Violet between the shoulder blades.

We all watched as the kittens joined the other cats chasing the remote control mice.

"We have to take them with us," Violet said. "We must help them find their real family."

We all piled into Pamela's Tarago with the Christmas presents just as the sun was rising. She had parked it up the street from Rita Raton's house, and the trip home took only half an hour rather than the epic three hours it had taken to get there. Cuddling the black kittens, who only minutes before had been Emily and Edward Raton, was a welcome distraction from the pain in my ankle.

Pamela explained that a Creature of Magic needed contact with cats to trigger a transformation and that if a child got to the age of ten without any cat contact, there was a chance they would lose their power to transform. Rita Raton's horror at poor Ginger's behaviour jumping on Emily now made sense. She had kept Emily and Edward away from cats to ensure they stayed in human form.

"But how did she take them?" Greta asked sleepily. "You can't just go around stealing people's children. Where are their parents, why aren't they looking for them?"

"They will be looking for them," Pamela clarified. "Most Creatures of Magic live in magical communities. But the Inquisitors have a very strong and complex network of kidnappers and non-magical people willing to look after kidnapped babies. Once the babies are taken from their magical parents it can be very difficult to track them down in the wider

219

non-magical community. Believe me, I know how hard it is to find your stolen baby."

She looked sadly at Violet.

"I was like Emily and Edward," Violet explained. "That's my Unfortunate Past."

"Violet was stolen when she was only a couple of months old, when we were at a museum in the Other Place," Pamela explained.

"No, Mum, it was here, not in the Other Place," Violet contradicted.

Pamela frowned. "Kitten, I think I know where it happened. I remember it very clearly, and you were only a couple of months old. We were in a museum. I was looking at a National Geographic display about native marsupial mice and then you were gone, lifted straight from the pram." In the rear vision mirror I saw Pamela's eyes well with tears at the memory.

"It took us eight years to find her, eight of the worst years of my life. We never stopped searching or hoping, and we were so scared we wouldn't find her before her tenth birthday."

Violet was still shocked. "I thought we were safe in the Other Place, Mother. I didn't want to come here because I thought we would be in more danger."

Suddenly, everything became clear to me. Violet *did* want to get caught. She had taken huge risks from the moment we met. She had forced Pamela to break the rules so her family would be sent back to the Other Place, where she felt safe.

I didn't know what to think or say.

"It might have been safe in the Other Place once, but not now," Pamela said. "Your father and I didn't want to scare you while we were there, but the way things are going it's probably safer here. At least here the Bureau is protecting us."

Tabitha piped up with an uncharacteristically pertinent comment. "Mum, I don't think the Bureau is doing a good job. I know Roger's away, but someone should have been filling in and tonight, well, if it hadn't been for you, we might still be in that cage."

"Yes," said Pamela, resting her chin on her hand.

I wanted to know more about Violet's Unfortunate Past.

"How?" I asked. "How did you find her?"

"It's a long story," said Pamela. "Too long to tell you now. Another time, when we don't have sprained ankles, transmogrified kittens and sleeping children to deal with."

I turned around – Greta was fast asleep. Edward and Emily were becoming restless and I realised that the sound and smell of the rabbit in its hutch in the back of the car was irresistible to their kitten noses.

"It probably wasn't the best choice of present for a Creature of Magic," Violet commented to her mother.

"No, kitten," Pamela agreed. "But I didn't know they were Creatures of Magic then."

"What are you going to do with Edward and Emily?" I asked. "Even though they were kidnapped themselves, you can't just kidnap them back now, can you?"

"Just watch me," Pamela said grimly.

"But what about Rita?" I asked. "She's not going to let them go."

"No," Pamela pondered. "I'm going to have to think about that. I've got a bit of time though. I told Cleo to leave her in the cage at least twelve hours before giving her the key."

❋

We pulled up outside our house. Pamela carried Greta out of the car and asked Violet to come and help her. Their plan was to put her to bed in Tabitha and Violet's room. In the morning Pamela would offer to collect her from the camp, as well as telling Mum and Dad that I had hurt my ankle falling down the stairs. Mum and Dad would probably be distracted enough by my ankle not to notice anything fishy was going on.

Even with the pain in my ankle I had trouble staying awake. It was all I could do to keep my eyes open while Violet and Pamela half-carried, half-walked me into their house.

26

Friend, *noun* **person you like and trust.**

I ended up in casualty at the hospital. Luckily, my ankle was badly sprained rather than broken.

Mum and Dad were surprisingly calm about it, although they were puzzled by my torn and dirty clothes. Greta's clothes were nearly as bad. I'm sure Mum would have had a few questions about what had happened at Guide Camp if she hadn't been so intent on looking after me. Greta had scratches on her legs from climbing the boulders in the national park, a graze on her head from one of the flying metal bars, and she was covered in mosquito bites. While I was at the hospital with Mum she had a shower and was looking reasonably presentable by the time we got back. She had plastered her mozzie bites with bandaids, which wasn't the best move given the attention it drew to them, but Mum didn't do more than raise an eyebrow and comment to Dad that they should have packed some insect repellent in Greta's backpack.

Pamela visited soon after we got home. I heard her downstairs, talking to Mum. "Thanks so much for that – I'm not sure if the holiday will happen, but if it does, it would be great if you could look after Oscar. I'll just go up and talk to Anna. There is a meditation trick I've learned to manage pain; I think it could help her."

Pamela's step on the stairs was light but the faint tinkle of her bell announced her arrival. She sat down on the bed beside me, smelling of strawberries and honey.

"How are you, kitten? How is your ankle?"

"It's okay," I said, shifting slightly under the covers.

"And how are you feeling after your foray into felininity?" she asked delicately. "There have been no lasting effects?"

It took me a moment to understand what she meant.

"Oh, you mean me being a cat! No, that's been okay – once Violet changed me back I was fine." A thought occurred to me. "Why, doesn't it always work?"

"It depends on the skill of the Creature doing the spell," Pamela explained. "With someone like Violet you can be confident that it will work well, but unfortunately, less skilled practitioners can experience difficulty."

"Difficulty?" I asked.

"You can get stuck halfway," Pamela explained, adding,

"you know, not quite cat, not quite human."

I made a mental note never to let Tabitha try any transmogrification on me.

"But I didn't come to talk to you about that," Pamela said. "I have some advice for you. I thought I should tell you now just in case we decide to go on a holiday, a long holiday." She drew her face close to mine and whispered, "Be careful of the people in the black robes."

I almost laughed. And then I thought back to the people in black robes Mum and I had noticed on the street, and the black figure in the tree that I had dismissed because of my poor eyesight and vivid imagination.

"They are Inquisitors, Anna. They have been watching and will continue to watch," Pamela continued seriously. "The best thing you can do is avoid them."

Inquisitors. I had read about them and seen them but no one had ever explained them to me. "Pamela, can you please tell me what these people are and what they are trying to do?"

"Traditionally, their mission was to destroy all Creatures of Magic. The tactics they use depends who is in charge at the time," Pamela said. "Arthur Raton's methods have been the cruellest we have seen to date. Mostly they're not the cleverest bunch, particularly the new recruits. They're people who like dressing up, who like belonging to a club with a bit of mystery, with a uniform to make them feel important and a mission to give them purpose. And then being told it is all a secret, I'm sure that's the clincher. That's why they parade in their black robes looking mysterious. There's no point having a secret unless everyone knows you have one and that you won't tell them what it is, or who you really are, and what you are trying to do."

I understood what Pamela was saying. "I've got a secret but I won't tell" is something lots of kids say. It's like waving a lolly in front of someone's face and then eating it yourself. The point is that you have something you are not going to share and that makes you feel powerful. It seemed adults could be the same, just not with lollies.

Pamela continued, "And there is nothing like a bit of hate and fear to bring people together. It's just unlucky for Creatures of Magic that we are what they hate and fear."

"So where do they find these people?" I asked.

"I don't know," said Pamela. She corrected herself. "I don't know how they recruit new members. Something to do with computers."

Pamela, like most of her family, had a very poor understanding of things technological. I wasn't sure whether she understood the concept of the internet.

"There are some very old Inquisitor families who have passed down the hate of Creatures of Magic from generation to generation. These ones tend to play an organisational role, like Rita Raton. But some of them have rebelled and rejected this inherited hate. They are not all bad." Her voice softened. "Some of them have even come to love Creatures."

"What about Arthur?" I asked. "Is he from an old Inquisitor family?"

"In a manner of speaking," Pamela said. "But Arthur is something else entirely. He is an experiment that went horribly wrong and the less you know about his history the better."

She would not budge on this.

I could hear Mum walking up the stairs and the soft tread of someone beside her. It was Violet.

Pamela stood up and stroked Violet's hair. "I'll go now. Goodbye, Anna, Dorothy — don't stay too long, Violet."

"Yes," Mum agreed. "Anna's tired and she needs to have some rest."

"Yes, I understand, Dorothy," Violet said seriously. "Sleep can be the best medicine. See you at home, Mother."

I giggled. At one time I would have found Violet's tone annoying but suddenly it didn't bother me any more.

"What?" asked Violet when Mum and Pamela had left. "Why

are you laughing?" She bent over to pick up my glasses from the floor, folded them up and put them in my glasses case on the bedside table.

"Nothing," I said. Then, trying to be honest without being insulting, I added, "Sometimes you sound like you are trying to be really mature. It sounds a bit fake, and kind of funny."

"Do you think I sound funny?" Violet asked. She wasn't insulted. I could tell she thought it was funny to be thought of as *being* funny.

"Kind of," I said.

Something had changed since our trip to the Ratons' house. Maybe it was Violet giving me her emblem, and then being cats together. Maybe it was finding out about Violet's Unfortunate Past and the real threat of the Inquisitors. I understood now that Violet was fighting a battle to protect her family and keep them safe. This was her priority. It didn't mean our friendship wasn't important but it meant sometimes she had bigger things to think about. I believed that she had tried to find help for me when I hurt my ankle, but something had gone wrong.

She seemed to read my mind.

"I was going for help, Anna, when Rita caught me. As soon as I was in cat form she seemed to know exactly where I was. She was waiting for me with a sack when I left the national park, and

I didn't have my emblem. She took me back to her house and there were dogs …" She shivered.

"You do believe me, Anna?" she asked in a small voice. "I only left you to get help. I didn't just leave you there and go straight to Rita's for the book."

Knowing that she cared about my believing her made me feel warm inside. She was the strangest friend I'd ever had. Yes, she sometimes sounded superior and kept a lot of stuff to herself, but being around her was exciting. With Violet around, life had become a kind of fairytale. She trusted me enough to let me into her world of magic and I knew now I could trust her to be my true friend, who would do anything to help me.

I reached over to hug her. "I believe you, Violet," I said. We sat in silence for a little while. It was the comfortable silence we often shared.

"Thanks for being my friend," Violet said softly as she left the room. "I'll let you sleep."

27

Shemozzle, *noun* tangle of messy events
that sometimes unravels into something good.

When I woke it was the middle of the night. It took a while to remember everything that had happened over the last couple of days. As I replayed the events in my mind I started to worry about Pamela and Violet.

I was scared of the Inquisitors, particularly Arthur. I couldn't imagine how Pamela could take Emily and Edward, in cat form or not, without expecting Rita Raton to come looking. Or maybe she knew she would come looking. Maybe she had a plan. Although without wanting to sound critical, planning did not seem to be Pamela's strong point. I remembered Pamela's mention of a long holiday. Was that how she was going to manage everything?

I looked out the window. The full moon of the last couple of nights was starting to wane and our backyard was full of shadows. There was a slight wind and it was catching at the plastic covering the swimming pool in the Browns' backyard, which was still at the hole-in-the-ground stage. I watched the plastic blow upwards, into a shape that resembled a black-robed figure. It moved slowly and my body tingled with fear — the plastic figure was not moving in the direction of the wind. I squinted and fumbled around on my bedside table for my glasses, which for once were where they should be. As I put them on my face with trembling fingers I mentally thanked Violet for being a neat freak. It was not plastic that was moving. Three hooded figures were making their way slowly through the Browns' yard. One of the figures was carrying a cat carry cage — the kind you would use to take your cat to the vet — and inside was a yowling, struggling tabby kitten. Orlando was clinging desperately to the robes of the Inquisitor. It must be Brendan in the cage! Was this a mistake? Were these Inquisitors intending to steal back Emily and Edward? Who was the second cat they were returning for? I remembered Pamela's comment: "mostly they're not the cleverest bunch." Orlando was crying, trying to pull the cage out of the Inquisitor's hand, and the Inquisitor pushed him roughly to the ground. I willed Orlando to scream but all he managed was a yowl of fear and rage.

I sprang into action, forgetting about my sprained ankle and cursing as I landed on it. I woke Greta — Brendan was

not her favourite person, but surely she would be able to look past his attempted eating of Fuzzy and help him. I explained the situation in a few hurried whispers. Greta pulled the attic ladder down and scrambled through the ceiling cavity to fetch Violet.

I could hear a whispered argument next door in Violet's room and mentally willed them to stop arguing and act. The Inquisitors were struggling with the Browns' back door. Pamela was pretty slack about security and didn't usually lock the door as there was a lot of midnight movement around their house. Thankfully, this was one night when the back door was locked. One of the hooded figures swore softly when he realised this. They looked around and pointed to a ladder leaning against the wall. It was the same rickety ladder that Greta had used to shelve the books, the one that at some stage had housed a colony of termites. Even though I didn't want him to get into the Browns' house, I felt a stab of fear for the Inquisitor who began climbing slowly up towards the bathroom window. He was watching his feet rather than looking to his destination, and his climbing was further complicated because he was holding a second, empty carry cage. He didn't see the figure leaning out the bathroom window, watching him.

"Sailor?" she asked, with a trill of excitement in her voice.

I heard Violet scream, "Yes, Charlene, sailor! Sing, Charlene, sing!"

The Inquisitor looked up and was met with the startling sight of Charlene in a bikini, her hair dangling Rapunzel-like out the window. She took a deep breath.

Charlene sang and all her pent up frustration was unleashed. It was loud, glorious and terrible. As I listened the world froze and every sound except Charlene's song was muted. In slow motion I saw the hooded Inquisitor falling through the collapsing rungs of the termite-ridden ladder, and the other Inquisitors pointing at Charlene before falling to the ground. Then Wocky leaped into the backyard, his slobbering jaw no longer slack but snarling. He landed on the Inquisitors and, responding to an order I couldn't hear, he attacked. I saw rather than heard the screams before I drifted into unconsciousness.

❋

I was unconscious for a full day after listening to Charlene's song. Pamela had quickly intervened and converted my Charlene-induced coma into a more natural sleep. Mum and Dad just assumed I was really tired after my sleepover and sprained ankle and accepted my long sleep as a natural response to exhaustion.

A couple of days later I hobbled over to the Browns' on my crutches. We all sat around the table in the family room at the back of the house.

Charlene was lying in the paddling pool in the sunniest part of the room, wearing sunglasses and drinking a cup of coffee. Wocky was lying at Tabitha's feet. Like the rest of the family he was becoming less nocturnal. It was strange, he showed absolutely no interest in the toy mice, Charlene, or even the Raton kittens who were frolicking around, but seemed very interested in Greta's mozzie bites, one of which she had been picking. He was growing positively animated, his slack lips tightening over his fanged teeth and a low sound that wasn't quite a bark escaping from his mouth. Greta was giggling but Violet whispered something to Tabitha, who sighed.

"Downstairs, Wocky," she ordered. Wocky slunk out, his tail between his legs. He looked over his shoulder and when he saw Violet and Tabitha weren't watching he lay down on the back doorstep.

"We were having fun!" Greta complained to Violet.

"Yes, until he starts to partake. Of you," Violet said pointedly. "He can smell your blood. Hunger is the best sauce, Greta. He's not a vegetarian and you're human so, just don't go there. You know what happened to the Inquisitors."

Greta stopped complaining. Violet filled me in for the umpteenth time on what had happened after I lost consciousness. You can never hear too many times how baddies, particularly baddies as bad as the Inquisitors, have been defeated, particularly if you played a role in their downfall.

Violet said that after Pamela made sure I was okay and released poor little Brendan (Greta rolled her eyes) she had dragged the Inquisitors into the cellar. Wocky was not kind to them while they had been unconscious and there had been a great deal of blood and stitching that took place in the privacy of the cellar. Violet said her father was a dab hand with a needle and we all agreed this was a useful skill to have.

After the Inquisitors had been repaired by John Brown with a non-magical needle and surgical thread (Pamela commented there had been enough magic used for the one day) there was an emergency meeting with a representative from the Bureau. With three unconscious, bloody although stitched up Inquisitors, two reclaimed Creature of Magic children and two potentially lethal magical creatures, all contained in the Browns' terrace, along with four children, lots of mice and any number of cats, both the Bureau and Pamela were understandably concerned about unwanted attention being drawn to her family in our non-magical neighbourhood. Given that it was the Bureau's job to protect the Browns from the Inquisitors, it reflected badly on them that they had failed to do this. This was lucky because it meant that the Bureau was helping (in a begrudging way) to cover up the questionable activities that had gone on that night. Or so they said.

It was decided that the Raton children would be handed over to the Bureau, which would take charge of liaising with the Other Place in the hope of finding their parents. Violet was confident that if they were alive, they would be found, because they would have registered their missing children and once Emily and Edward were safely back in a magical community, magic could be used to track their family anyway.

Violet wasn't sure what had happened to the Inquisitors. One was Rita Raton and the others were known to the Bureau but not the Browns. Arthur Raton was not one of them. Once they had been restored to consciousness a lot of arguing and shouting had gone on in the cellar, between Pamela, the Bureau and the Inquisitors. Some agreement must have been reached because in the early hours of the following morning, the Inquisitors left the Browns' house with their empty cat cages, escorted by the Bureau in their official vehicle (a shabby-looking taxi with a permanently engaged light). Violet said her mother had been tightlipped about what had taken place. Apparently, all the magic Pamela had used to rescue her children and Emily and Edward was serious stuff. She had broken any number of magical laws and Violet said there would definitely be consequences, it was just a matter of how severe these consequences would be. Like her mother, she was reluctant to elaborate.

I asked Violet something that had been puzzling me since our visit to Rita Raton's. "Why did you stay in the cage when Rita put you there? Why didn't you use magic to escape?"

"I was scared," Violet said simply. "The dogs scared me. In cat form I couldn't get past my fear. It made me forget I could perform magic, and I didn't have my emblem to remind me."

Wocky had crept back inside. He growled and Violet patted him gently.

"Wocky doesn't like the word 'dog' any more than we do," she said. "But getting back to that night. Magic is a bit like meditating. You have to relax into it and make your mind calm. When you're frozen with fear it's very difficult."

I digested this information and moved my foot to dodge an accelerating remote control mouse operated by Brendan.

Orlando and Brendan had taken charge of most of Emily and Edward's Christmas presents, riding the scooters, playing with the train and responsibly looking after the rabbit. (I had been worried about the boys changing into kittens and doing something dreadful to the rabbit, but they had been great.) Brendan hadn't transmogrified since his stint in the cat cage, and Orlando had said his first word: "cat". In marked contrast, Emily and Edward had not changed back into human form since their transmogrification at the Ratons' house. The Browns accepted this as fairly standard for small children who had just discovered their magical status.

"The novelty will wear off soon enough," Pamela said indulgently, sending Violet down to the butcher for extra chicken necks and mince.

As children, Edward and Emily had been unnaturally good. As kittens they were appropriately mischievous. They were chasing the remote control mice as Brendan and Orlando manoeuvred them across the floor when there was a loud knock at the front door.

"I'll get it, Mum," Tabitha called out.

Later I wished she hadn't.

28

Bureau, *noun* an organisation or a business that collects or provides information. Sometimes this type of organisation has trouble with efficient enactment of their designated duties.

Tabitha walked into the family room with Roger. Although he looked tanned from his recent holiday he was wearing a suit, which was unusual. His mustache had been trimmed. He wore his suit with the lack of conviction that had characterised his disguises. I realised later we had confused Roger's disguises with who he really was. He was not a removalist or builder. When Brendan and Orlando ran up to him and rummaged in his pockets for lollies he gently pushed them away. He cleared his throat and if a look of sadness crossed his face it was only for a moment.

"Roger!" said Pamela, walking forwards with both arms outstretched. "To what do we owe this pleasure? How was your holiday, and how is Olivia?"

"Mum, I don't think he's here to talk about his holiday,"

said Violet, taking Pamela's hand in hers.

Roger took no one's hand. "Pammy, I'm here on business, official Bureau business and I think it's best for everyone if we just go by the book. And you might want the children to leave the room."

Pamela dropped her arms. Her voice wobbled but was clear. "Brendan and Orlando, could you please take the Raton kittens outside for a play? Uncle Roger and I have a few things to discuss."

The boys must have sensed something in Pamela's tone. For once they did as they were told, scooping Edward and Emily into their arms and going out into the backyard.

"And the girls, Pammy?" Roger asked.

"They can stay, Roger. They need to hear the truth – they need to hear directly from the Bureau what's what."

"As you wish, Pammy," he said. He squared his shoulders as if to brace himself. "It's not good news, love. It's not Siberia but it's somewhere a bit colder and it's all of you. Minimum four months, maximum three years, and the mermaid will be locked up. The dog, I'm afraid—"

"Wocky is not a dog," Tabitha said, obviously frustrated by the stupidity of grown-ups.

Wocky growled.

"Wocky, cellar!" Pamela ordered.

Wocky shuffled out the back, his claws scratching the floorboards.

"And Tabitha, no more interruptions," said Pamela. She turned to Roger with trepidation.

Roger cleared his throat and looked Pamela directly in the eye. He did not look at the children. "The dog needs to be destroyed."

"Destroyed?" Tabitha asked. With a wobbling voice she managed to pull out a number of synonyms. "You mean put down, sentenced to death, killed?"

At that moment the key turned in the door and John Brown walked in. He'd performed at an afternoon concert and judging from the spring in his step it had gone well.

"Hello, girls. Hi, Pamela. And Roger — good to see you, Roger!" he held out his hand to Roger who shook it stiffly.

"I was just explaining to Pammy that I am here strictly in an official capacity so to speak, John," Roger explained.

"Why the formality, Roger?" asked John Brown. He looked from Pamela to Violet and Tabitha and then me and Greta and the sombre mood in the room seemed to dawn on him.

Pamela reached over and took John's hand.

"John," she said gently, holding his hand. "John, I'm afraid Roger has some bad news for us."

245

"What?" asked John Brown. "Pamela, has someone died?"

"Not yet," piped Tabitha.

Roger took over.

"John, all that's been going on in the last couple of days, the injuries that Wocky and Charlene inflicted on the Inquisitors, the fact they are even here, what went down at the Ratons ... It doesn't look good, mate. I'm sorry I wasn't here for it all, I am, but the fact is I wasn't. And the report has been written, the die is cast so to speak. So let's keep it all official and not make a fuss. Pammy broke the rules, and Wocky, well, Wocky nearly killed those people and there's a price that's got to be paid, John."

John Brown's eyes widened. He didn't say anything.

Pamela spoke directly to her husband. "John, what Roger is saying is that Wocky will be put down."

John Brown gave a cry of anguish. "No, not my Wocky! Surely not, Roger, surely not!" And to my surprise a tear trickled down his cheek. Pamela stroked his hand.

Roger looked at John Brown and when he spoke it was in the impersonal tone of someone distancing themselves from a familiar but distasteful script.

"Yes, John, Wocky will be destroyed. I have the van waiting outside to take him away. I'm taking Charlene too."

I shot a look at Pamela and was surprised at what I saw. She looked angry, very angry, and as scary as when the metal bars flew across the room in Rita Raton's house. Tabitha for once was silent.

Pamela tossed her hair. At least she attempted to toss it. Really curly hair like Pamela's does not toss well, it just vibrates or wobbles. She nonetheless threw her curly head of hair back, drew herself up to her full height and spoke clearly in a voice that resonated with anger.

"Well, if it's going to be official, Roger, let's keep it official. The first thing is the name is *Pamela*, not Pammy," she said. She glared at Roger and he did not shrink from the gaze.

"Okay, Pamela, my girl," he said. "Point taken, the name is Pamela." He pulled out a piece of paper and glanced at it before attempting to pass it to Pamela. She did not take it and after a moment he drew his hand back.

"And another thing, Roger, I am a woman, not a girl, but a woman," she said in icy tones. "I am a woman called Pamela, who happens to be a witch."

"Um, Creature of Magic, Mum," Tabitha said, her momentary silence proving to be just that.

"Let's call things what they are for once," Pamela said in ringing tones. "I am a witch. I have children who are often cats, children with a talent for magic and some who are simply very brave. We are not perfect, and I am not denying we have made some mistakes. But, Roger, quite frankly you can like it or lump it. I'm through with all this subterfuge. As we have demonstrated …"

(At this point, Violet snuggled up to her mother because of her collaborative use of "we".)

"Yes, as we have demonstrated," pronounced Pamela. You could tell she was really warming to her theme. You could almost hear the drum roll. "We are simply not prepared to be victims and stand idly by while these vile, vile people persecute us. These people have STOLEN our children. They have crept uninvited into our world and *stolen* our children and you expect us to just take it! You tie our hands so we can't protect them in the way we know best, and promise that you will protect us, but you don't! You failed, Roger, it is you and the Bureau who have let me and my family and my species down, but you have the gall to stand there and tell me that I am going to be punished for your failings! What was I supposed to do, Roger? Stand by and let them take my family, lock up my children and make them miserable? They have done it once, but I swear I will not let them do it again, ever, and if that means I break every law governing non-magical and Creature of Magic interaction, I will break them!"

She glared at him, green eyes glinting, every curly hair on her head standing up as though she had been electrocuted.

Roger was not deterred. "Sorry, Pamela," he said stiffly. "I'm just doing my job, love. Nothing personal as you know."

He cleared his throat and read from the piece of paper.

"Under the power vested in me by the Bureau for the Protection of Creatures of Magic, you, Pamela Brown, as a Creature of Magic, are charged with the following offences under the *Charter of Magical Doings, 1300*:

1. Summoning of magical creature without a permit;

2. Keeping magical creatures without a permit;

3. Transmogrification with intent to harm;

4. Transmogrification of a human child;

5. Entering into a conspiracy to cover up magic with a human child.

"You are ordered into exile, effective immediately. Any members of your family that choose to accompany you to said exile in Antarctica shall be free to do so."

There was stunned silence and even Pamela went pale. Her hair drooped and her shoulders hunched slightly. Only Violet looked unperturbed.

It was John Brown who broke the silence, speaking for the first time since being told of Wocky's death sentence. His voice was surprisingly steady.

"Well, I suppose we'd better start packing then. I must say that my life back in the non-magical community has been

disappointing. But, Roger, if we all leave without a fuss, you must let us bring Wocky and Charlene. You have my word I will not let him harm any human. Surely you cannot be so unjust as to punish, or kill, our pet and friend for following our instructions."

"Yes," said Violet, speaking for the first time. "I told Charlene to sing and Wocky to attack. Punish us—"

"He is, Vi, he is," said Tabitha.

"But not Wocky and Charlene," finished Violet, ignoring Tabitha.

"I can put it to the Bureau," said Roger. "But you know I can't promise anything."

"No," said John Brown, firmly. "Don't put it to the Bureau, just let them come, for the sake of our families' friendship, Roger. I promise we will all be ready to leave tonight, and leave without incident, but Wocky and Charlene need to come too."

There was a long silence.

Roger looked from John Brown to Pamela to Violet, across to Tabitha and back to John Brown.

"Eleven o'clock sharp," he said. "There will be a vehicle with a cage, a water therapy tank and room for your family. Now, no funny business, all right?"

He shook John Brown's and Pamela's hands and after a curt nod to us all he was gone.

251

29

Melancholy, *noun* a fog rather
than storm of sadness.

The Browns left that night. After Roger left, Pamela had briskly sent us home and I scarcely had time to say goodbye to Violet or Tabitha.

Greta climbed up into the attic to watch them leave, but I couldn't even manage this with my ankle. Greta said that the cats of the street made a guard of honour for the large truck that came in the middle of the night. Even Ginger left my bed to go down there, but I didn't begrudge him his loyalty to the Browns. Ginger had stuck to me like glue since my return from Rita Raton's house and I often caught him looking at me in a knowing kind of way. I think some part of him sensed the adventure I had been on and my new understanding of cats. So when Ginger looked at me as he leaped from my bed I knew that he was saying he would be back shortly and that really he was saying goodbye for both of us.

The only bright spot over the next few days was the present Ginger brought back from his farewell to the Browns — little Oscar the kitten. He had a note attached to his collar. It was in Violet's handwriting and it asked me to take care of Oscar until her return. Ginger was surprisingly welcoming to Oscar. He seemed to know that Oscar was just as much a victim of the Inquisitors' persecution as the Browns. They slept together every night at the end of my bed.

It was Mum who heard first from the Browns. She came in to sit on my bed. My ankle was still sore and apart from going downstairs to check the letterbox I hadn't been moving very much. Mum beat me to the letterbox that day, and as she sat down she pulled out a postcard. I recognised the writing as Pamela's.

"What does she say, Mum?" I asked eagerly.

"They've gone on a holiday," Mum answered. "A long holiday. Pamela doesn't know when they'll be back, or, reading between the lines, if they'll be back at all. If I didn't know them better, I'd think they were running away from some kind of trouble."

I had been hoping at least that Pamela would give Mum an address so I could write to Violet.

"They're in Antarctica," said Mum, puzzled. "It seems a

strange choice of holiday for a family that hates the cold, and water for that matter. Here, read it yourself."

I took the postcard from Mum and read:

Dearest Dorothy, Michael, Anna and Greta,

We are taking a break from the summer heat and have travelled to Antarctica. Thank you for being such good neighbours to us, and particularly to your girls for being such loyal and brave friends to our family. I am sorry we weren't able to say goodbye in person but there simply wasn't time. Violet said she will send word to Anna herself soon.

Love and best wishes

Pamela

"It all sounds very strange," Mum mused. "What does she mean by 'loyal and brave friends'?"

My eyes felt all hot and stingy and I had to blink.

Mum looked away. "School starts back next week," she said brightly. "Which means Lydia will be back any day now. Dear, that's come around quickly, hasn't it? We should go shopping for your new schoolbooks."

I knew Mum was trying to make me feel better — I love stationery — but even the thought of a stationery buying trip didn't help the sad feeling I had in my stomach.

"You go," I said. "I'd rather stay here. I feel tired and my ankle is still hurting."

"Okay," Mum said, getting up from the bed. "Do you want me to bring you anything?"

"No," I said, snuggling back down into bed. She was being so nice but it didn't make me feel any better. In fact it made me feel worse. Sometimes when someone is kind to you when you are feeling sad it just makes you feel sadder. My eyes were prickling again and I closed them and didn't open them again until Mum had left the room. Ginger looked at me from the end of the bed. I didn't mind Ginger seeing me cry; animals are good like that. They understand when you are sad but they don't need to talk about it.

I missed Violet. It had taken the whole school holidays for me to work her out, to realise I could trust her and to understand that she had been working to a bigger plan I had not always understood. School with Violet would have been the best. I had been hoping we would be in the same class and was dying for Violet to meet my friends, particularly Lydia.

I looked out my window wearily. The black plastic covering the hole in the Browns' backyard had been weighed down with bricks. It looked desolate. There would be no pool parties now. There would probably not even be a pool, just a big hole in the ground that would eventually become muddy and smelly with the rain, a breeding ground for super mosquitoes that would fly through Greta's and my window and bite us throughout the night.

The sky was grey with low-lying clouds. It would probably rain soon. It took me a while to notice the white writing. A layer of whiter clouds started to form letters over the grey sky. A shaky "G" and then an "R" formed, followed by an "EETINGS", a space then "ANNA". My heart thumped and I sat upright in bed, waiting eagerly for the rest of the message. It slowly appeared.

GREETINGS ANNA I WILL BE BACK FOR SCHOOL IN TERM 2 MISS YOU

Violet would be back. Soon.

257

ACKNOWLEDGEMENTS

Thanks to Anna for help getting started, Zoe and Claire for reading each chapter as it was written, all the Gradys, particularly Mum and Dad for their encouragement and support, the Fenton-Smiths for their inspirational love of cats, Barbara Mobbs for opening the door to the publishing world, my editor Nicola Robinson for pulling *Creatures of Magic* into a cohesive whole, Amy Daoud for her beautiful cover design, Lilly Piri for her illustrations and lastly Will whose love and support in clearing a space in our lives for writing made this book possible.

ABOUT THE AUTHOR

MAREE FENTON-SMITH grew up in Wagga Wagga in south-western New South Wales with four siblings, two parents and lots of animals. She studied English and Social Work at university and now lives in the inner west in Sydney with four children, one husband and a cat called Rosebud. *Creatures of Magic* is her first novel.

ABOUT THE ILLUSTRATOR

LILLY PIRI is a visual artist and illustrator from Queensland, Australia. She moved to Germany in 2007, and wandered home in 2011, with three solo exhibitions and fluent Deutsch under her belt. Her work has been featured in *Frankie, Yen, Empty, Semi-Permanent, Curvy,* and she has worked with clients like Oxfam America, MILK Japan, Poketo, *Harper's Bazaar,* Iron Fist, and Saatchi & Saatchi. She is represented by the Jacky Winter group, in Melbourne, and Retrospect Galleries, in Byron Bay.

MORE GREAT FICTION

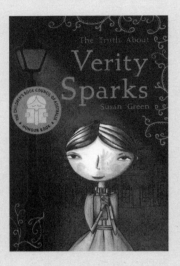

London. 1878.

Verity Sparks has an extraordinary talent: she can find lost things just by thinking about them.

When she joins a Confidential Inquiry Agency, she discovers there is a mystery lurking in her own past and that unknown forces are working against her. It soon becomes clear that Verity and her friends are in great danger.

Who doesn't want them to learn the truth about Verity Sparks?

The Truth About Verity Sparks was awarded Honour Book for Younger Readers, CBCA Book of the Year Awards, 2012

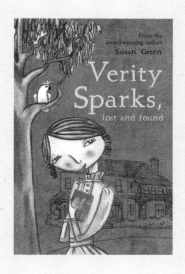

Melbourne. 1879.

Verity Sparks has found her father. But she has lost her gift – the ability to find lost things.

Papa Savinov, eager for Verity to become a proper lady, sends her to the exclusive boarding school Hightop House. But Verity is more interested in solving the case of the missing Ecclethorpe heiress.

As the investigation deepens, danger and intrigue grow closer. Will Verity's gift return before it's too late?

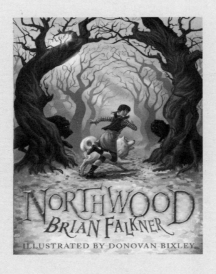

Cecilia Undergarment likes a challenge.

So when she discovers a sad and neglected dog, she is determined to rescue him.

But her daring dog rescue lands her lost and alone in the dark forest of Northwood.

A forest where ferocious black lions roam.

A forest where those who enter never return.

But then, Northwood has never seen the likes of Cecilia Undergarment before …

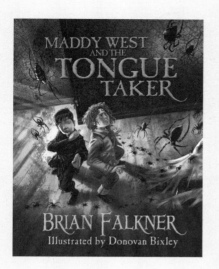

Maddy West can speak every language in the world.

When she is asked to translate some ancient scrolls, Maddy is excited.

But the scrolls hide many secrets.

Secrets that send Maddy on a wild adventure with a stowaway ninja, a mysterious monkey, a Bulgarian wrestler, and a fiendish witch.

And soon Maddy finds herself in deadly peril.

Does Maddy have what it takes to save herself and her new friends?

In the
wings

ELSBETH
EDGAR

Ella Jamison dreams of acting.

But it's an impossible dream when
you suffer from stage fright.

Stuck in the backstage crew for the
school play, *A Midsummer Night's
Dream*, Ella watches her friends and
conceited new boy, Sam, tread the
boards. But first impressions can be
deceiving. And help can arrive when
you least expect it.

When Cassie and Liam start swimming at the lake neither of them realises the dark secrets that lie beneath.

As summer heats up and the lake waters become lower and lower, a shocking truth is slowly uncovered.

And soon, both their lives will change – forever.

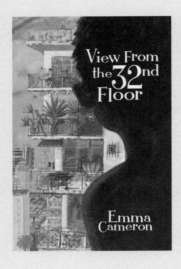

Something special has been gifted to you. Join your neighbours, Saturday, 6.00 pm, on the roof.

Living on the thirty-second floor of an apartment block, William has a clear view of the building opposite. He sees his neighbours eating ice-cream, watering potted palms, painting pictures … or as shadows behind closed curtains.

Shadows worry William. With his new friend Rebecca, and helped by lots of cake, a dictionary of names, tai chi, and banana-shaped sticky notes, he plans to tempt his lonely neighbours back into the world.

Can they succeed? Always always.

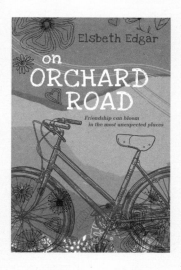

A new baby sister.

A new school.

A new town.

Jane is sure that she will be miserable.

But sometimes friendship can bloom in the most unexpected places.